THE VOICE INSIDE MY HEAD

S.J. LAIDLAW

Tundra Books

Text copyright © 2014 by S.J. Laidlaw

Published in Canada by Tundra Books,
a division of Random House of Canada Limited,
One Toronto Street, Suite 300, Toronto, Ontario M5C 2V6

Published in the United States by Tundra Books of Northern New York,
P.O. Box 1030, Plattsburgh, New York 12901

Library of Congress Control Number: 2013936989

Library and Archives Canada Cataloguing in Publication

Laidlaw, S.J., author
The voice inside my head / by S.J. Laidlaw.

Issued in print and electronic formats.
ISBN 978-1-77049-565-4 (bound).—ISBN 978-1-77049-566-1 (ebook)

I. Title.

PS8623.A394V64 2014   jC813'.6   C2013-902296-1
                                               C2013-902297-X

Edited by Sue Tate
Designed by Kelly Hill

Text images by Katerina Kirilova/Shutterstock.com

www.tundrabooks.com

Printed and bound in the United States of America

1 2 3 4 5 6   19 18 17 16 15 14

ACKNOWLEDGMENTS

I've been uniquely blessed to benefit from the wisdom and talent of several women. First among them is Sue Tate, my editor at Tundra Books, whose meticulous editorial skills are only surpassed by her warmth and compassion.

Second is my former agent, Andrea Cascardi. I wasn't at all surprised when she decided to return to editing because she was always the best combination an author could hope for, a truly gifted editorial agent.

Third are my friends at MiG Writers, who continue to accompany me on the writing journey as we savor the successes and share the angst. It would be a lonelier world without them.

As always, I want to thank my husband, Richard, who not only supports my writing but didn't balk when I told him I wanted to buy a home on a tiny island off the coast of Honduras.

Finally, I owe a debt of gratitude to my parents that I can never repay. To my mother, who is still the most determined woman I know and taught me to read, despite my dyslexia, confidently assuring me I would one day become a writer. And to my father, who shared his own passion for books and talent for writing, and who, for many years, long after his passing, was the voice inside my head.

THE

VOICE

INSIDE

MY

HEAD

CHAPTER 1

You know that moment when you spot a gorgeous girl across a room and just as you're working out your opening line, you realize she's checking you out and it's like every atom in the universe has lined up to create this one perfect connection?

Only then it turns out the room is actually a cramped, stifling cabin on a ferry heading to an island off the coast of Honduras, where your sister has disappeared. And you know the authorities might be right — she could have drowned, or got eaten by a shark, or fallen into the hands of South American drug lords — so you start to wonder what kind of person thinks about getting laid when his sister might be dead, or worse. Okay, so maybe you've never experienced that exact scenario, but you can see how it might be a buzz kill.

I turn away from the vision of perfection because all I see now is the face of my sister and I talk to her in my head. I continue the conversation we've been having for the past two weeks. I'll admit right up front that I'm filling in her lines; when you live with someone as opinionated as my sister, it's not hard to hear her telling you off, even when she's not there.

ME: *If you're not dead, I'll give up weed. I know I told you I'd already stopped, but that was a lie. This time I really will.*

PAT: *You're such a liar.*

ME: *This time I mean it, and I won't cut class anymore either.*

PAT: *I thought you'd stopped cutting class. The school didn't call home once last semester.*

ME: *Yeah, about that, they sort of got a note from Mom saying I had mono.*

PAT: *You never had mono.*

ME:

PAT: *You wrote that note yourself? You're unbelievable!*

"Ach!"

I look at the wet, yellow goo that has just landed on my shorts and the little kid sitting next to me who put it there. He stares at me with ginormous brown eyes, like he's as surprised as I am to find me covered in barf. His mom leans over and swipes at my shorts with a cloth, which rubs more of it in than off, while the kid edges away from me. Puke-stench soaks the already fetid air as the boat continues to rock violently and my stomach rocks right along with it. I fish my water bottle out of my pack and take a swig. Puke-kid looks at it longingly.

"I better not see this on my shorts, buddy," I say, before handing it over.

He continues the big-eyed stare as he drains my bottle. His mom smiles gratefully. She says something in Spanish, which I don't understand because Spanish followed Study Hall last year, and Jamie McCredie and I did a lot more weed than studying.

"Are you going to Utila?"

I look up in surprise to see the gorgeous girl has made her way to my side of the boat and is swaying over me, her long blond hair brushing my shoulder as she grabs the back of my seat to steady herself. She has an accent; Swedish maybe. That would just figure. The one time in my entire life I get hit on by a hot Swedish girl and I can't complete the play because I'm obsessing on my sister.

"Yeah," I say.

"I'm Birgit." She smiles.

"Luke." I don't smile.

She notices my lack of enthusiasm. I expect this is a unique experience in her world, where guys drop at her feet like bugs hitting a zapper.

"You don't sound happy," she says.

"I'm great." I show her my teeth.

"So why are you going to Utila?"

I doubt she'd be this persistently friendly if she felt she had easier options. We're on a boat with about forty Hondurans, crowded onto benches built for half that number, with only one other guy who looks like a fellow tourist. Judging by his bleary-eyed stare, he's not up for chit-chat.

"I was just going to ask you the same thing." I wasn't, but it beats telling her my own life story.

"It's supposed to be beautiful," she gushes, "and I've heard the diving's amazing. I want to snorkel with the whale sharks."

I'm bored.

Hot Swedish chick is boring me.

I don't want to hear about beauty, or diving, and I sure as heck don't want to hear about whale sharks.

"My sister works at the Whale Shark Research Center."
Damn! I specifically don't want to talk about my sister. Why
can't I keep my mouth shut?

"Really?" says Swedish chick, with way too much interest. "That's amazing. I'd love to meet your sister."

Now what? I really don't want to explain about Pat's disappearance to a stranger. The truth is, every time I talk about
her, I get a pain in my gut. Sometimes it's all I can do not to
throw up. I'm already feeling boat-queasy, so I definitely
don't want to take any chances. I stare out the window. Maybe
if I ignore this girl, she'll take the hint and go away.

The boat lurches.

Swedish chick falls into my lap.

Not making progress here.

God, she smells good. How does she do that in this heat?
Her hair is tickling my face. She shifts in my lap so she's
facing me and says something like "Oooplah," which makes
no sense whatsoever but sounds unbelievably cute. At the
same moment, we both stiffen, though not in the same way.

I'm sure there's some special hell reserved for guys who
get turned on even when they're on a quest to find their missing sisters. Come to think of it, maybe this is it.

Spanish lady gives me a disapproving look, like I engi-
neered this situation. She pulls puke-kid onto her lap. It's not
clear if she's trying to get him away from me or making space
for Swedish chick. Whatever the case, Swedish chick wriggles
off and squeezes in beside me, which theoretically is a good
thing but definitely not helpful under the circumstances.

"How old are you?" she asks, darting a look at my lap
like she needs to confirm the evidence.

"Seventeen," I admit.

"You look older." She sounds disappointed.

I get that a lot. I've been over six feet since I hit high school, and working construction this summer, I've bulked up. I guess I should be happy I look older. It's an advantage for attracting girls, but this isn't the first time someone's expected more from me than I can deliver.

"I'm twenty," she offers. "An old lady to you." She smiles smugly. She knows there isn't a guy on the planet who would think of her as old. Unattainable, yes. Old, no.

"Do you have a girlfriend?" she asks in a patronizing tone reserved for little brothers and other lower life forms.

"Yeah," I say, giving her a cool look. "She's twenty-two."

I immediately regret the lie. Not that I have a problem with lying, but I don't like to be pushed into it.

"Hey, dude!" It's the bleary-eyed guy, weaving unsteadily toward us. I guess I should have figured he'd migrate over eventually, but I'm amazed to see him upright. "You didn't tell me you were catching this ferry!" He stops just in front of us and runs a hand through long frizzy hair, which is only marginally redder than his eyes.

"Hello, miss." He gives Swedish chick a friendly smile and burps. She eyeballs him disdainfully. "You wouldn't mind finding another seat so I can sit with my man here, would you?"

She purses her luscious lips and turns to me. I think fast. Do I go with snotty Swedish chick or crazy stoner guy? It's no contest, really.

"Great to see you, man," I say. He holds out his knuckles and I knock them with my own.

"Cosmic," he says.

Swedish chick shrugs.

"Good luck," she says, scrambling over me to get out of her seat. I don't know which one of us she's talking to so I don't answer.

"Live long and prosper," says stoner guy, as she pushes past him. "Move over, dude," he says to me. "Good thing I was here to bail you out." He heaves a bulging pack off his back and settles into the narrow space I've just vacated. Swinging the pack onto his knees, he begins rifling through it, talking the whole time. "That girl was so not into you, man, and who needs that kind of action, right?" He belches loudly and Spanish lady clicks her tongue. "I almost missed this ferry. Three-day vacation on the mainland, like that's a vacation. Where the heck . . . ?" He stretches out the opening of his pack and stares into it. "Yes!" Grinning, he slides his hand deep into the bag and pulls out a beer, hands it to me and fishes out another. Uncapping it with his teeth, he trades it for the unopened one I'm holding and cracks that one, too.

"Are we allowed to drink on this boat?" I ask. Aside from the fact that it's eight in the morning, I really can't afford any trouble right now.

"This is Honduras, man." He seems to think that answers my question. Maybe it does.

"So, who are you, anyway?" I try to sound casual, like I don't notice his shirt's on inside out and he smells like he hasn't showered in days.

He gives a half-smile (perhaps he's not as clueless as he seems) and chugs at least three-quarters of his beer in one go. Another time, this would impress me.

Okay, I'll be honest, it does impress me.

"I'm Zach," he says, his smile fading as he starts picking at the label of his beer. For a moment I think he's going to say something more, but he just sighs, polishes off the dregs and starts rummaging in his bag again.

"Damn, I was sure I had one more in here." He turns to me as if I might have an explanation, which I'm pretty sure I do. I hold up my beer.

"Ohhh," he says slowly. "Gotcha." He puts his bag on the floor and slumps back in his seat. "I'm supposed to stop drinking, anyway. The boss gave me a couple of days off to dry out. That's why I went to the mainland. I figure if he doesn't see me drinking, it doesn't count, right?"

"You can have it back," I offer. "I haven't touched it."

"No, that's okay." He leans in and whispers confidentially, "I had a couple before I got on the boat." The smell of his breath makes my stomach twist.

"Yeah? Never would have guessed."

He grins. "I've always been like that; I can be totally wasted and people never know."

"Huh. So, if you don't mind me asking, how did you manage a couple of beers before we sailed? We left at 7:00 a.m."

He looks at me for a moment, before emitting another malodorous belch. "You're wondering how I could've been drinking so early?"

I nod and try breathing through my mouth.

"I wasn't drinking *early*." He pauses. "I was drinking *late*. I started last night and I only finished this morning."

I don't point out that technically he hasn't finished yet. I just hand over my beer.

"Thanks, man." He takes a long swig, rests the bottle on his knee and immediately tears up.

"Are you okay?" I'm a little rattled by his sudden mood swings, though I'm not one to talk. Since Pat's disappearance, my own moods have been all over the place.

"Nah, not really." He sighs. "I'm in mourning. A friend of mine drowned last week." He looks at me sadly, waiting for me to ask him about it.

I don't. In fact, I madly try to think of some way to change the subject.

I know he's talking about Pat. The island we're heading for has a total area of seventeen square miles, three-quarters of it wetlands and mangrove swamp. The population, crammed into one tiny corner, makes up a staggering six thousand people. And with all those people, the last drowning they had, other than the alleged drowning of my sister, was a beached whale, over a year ago. I did my homework. And I'm not discussing Pat with this alcoholic headcase.

"Her name was Tricia." Apparently, he's going to tell me anyway. "She was beautiful. She had this amazing black hair, like shoe polish or really shiny black stones, and green eyes, like grass but not dried-out grass, fresh grass, like in spring-time. And when she looked at you with those spring-grass eyes, it was like she saw you were a good person and not some loser whose own mother kicked him out just because he hit her boyfriend, who totally deserved it, and he was the loser, not me. You know what I mean?"

I twist the strap of my backpack around my fist.

First of all, no one calls her Tricia, and it's not like they haven't tried. With a name like Patricia it could go either way, and she's cheerleader pretty, so there's always some guy who thinks Tricia sounds cutesy, but Pat terminates those guys like they're enemy combatants. Second, I know exactly what he means. Pat's not just a good person. She's so relentlessly, optimistically good, she makes everyone around her want to try harder. I wouldn't say she succeeded where I am concerned, but as long as she's there, I feel there's hope.

"So were you close friends?" I ask. I don't really want to hear how my sister deserted our family so she could go help some other messed-up kid sort out his life, but I can't help but feel sorry for the guy. He's clearly miserable, and one way or another it's Pat's fault. Since she's not here, it kind of makes it my responsibility.

"The best," he says enthusiastically. "She was my best friend. Whenever we went drinking, she would always make sure I got home safely, and she never laughed at me, not once."

I sit up straight and stare at him. We have to be talking about different girls. My sister doesn't drink. She's the poster child for responsible living: no alcohol, no drugs, no sex. I used to say no life. But that joke's not so funny anymore.

"So what happened to your friend?" I demand, trying to keep the eagerness out of my voice.

"That's the thing, man, no one knows. One minute she was there, partying with the rest of us, and the next minute she's gone. Poof. No one saw her leave or anything. The police say she drowned, but I don't think so."

Ditto.

I didn't believe it for a second when my parents came back from Utila with a police report claiming my sister had drowned. They went through the whole report with me, pointing out that her clothes were found at the end of a dock, like she'd stripped off to go swimming. That part was believable. And apparently there was rain the night she disappeared so the waves may have been high. I don't think she would have gone in the water on a really stormy night, but that too is possible. Pat's a strong swimmer. It really would have depended on how bad the weather was, and the report wasn't very specific.

I don't deny she's missing. No one's seen her for more than two weeks, and all her belongings are still in her room, except for the clothes they found on the dock. But she's far more likely to have been kidnapped or gotten lost in the jungle. Unfortunately, the authorities are so satisfied with their bogus drowning scenario that they aren't even looking anymore. Ergo the road trip. Well, not road exactly. But someone needs to search for my sister. If the authorities won't, then I will.

"What do you think happened to her?" I ask.

"Dunno. Duppy, maybe."

"Duppy?"

"Yeah, like a ghost. You know. The island's full of 'em. It was a Mayan burial ground a long time ago."

"Utila?"

"Damn straight."

"The whole island was a Mayan burial ground?" This guy is either messing with me or completely insane.

"Word. The Maya brought their dead bodies from the mainland. They wanted 'em far away. Let 'em roam 'round their own island. You get what I'm saying?"

"So you think a Mayan ghost got your friend?"

"Makes more sense than drowning. She worked with sharks, man. She was totally seaworthy, if you get my drift."

He *is* talking about my sister. I've seen Pat swim in all kinds of weather, in oceans, in fast-moving rivers. She's obsessed with the water and everything that lives in it. Sometimes I think she's half-fish. It's a passion I neither share nor appreciate. But the partying and the nickname don't add up.

"Have you lived on the island very long?"

"About eight months. After my mom kicked me out, I bummed around Arizona for a while; that's where I'm from. Then I picked up some fake ID and started hitchhiking south. I didn't know where I was headed, but you could do a lot worse than Utila. The locals speak English, unlike the rest of Honduras. It was settled by some British dudes in the eighteen hundreds who migrated over from the Caymans. Now it's a real mix of people, though. A lot of mainlanders have moved over and people from other parts of the Caribbean. And there are tons of foreign kids from pretty much every country you could name. Most come for the diving and don't plan on staying more than a few weeks, but they usually end up hanging around a lot longer. It's that kind of place — easy to pick up work, crazy cheap if you aren't too fussy and really laid back. I can't explain it, but it grows on you. You'll see. In fact, there it is!"

I follow where he's pointing and just coming into view is an island. On one end, brightly painted wooden houses are crammed together, with a small hill rising behind them. There's not a single building higher than the towering palm and fruit trees that compete for every inch of open space. A narrow cut in the landmass separates the village from the rest of the island, which is miles of narrow, white-sand beach fronting towering, overgrown jungle. If Pat got lost in that, how am I ever going to find her?

CHAPTER 2

I try to shake Zach when I get off the boat. I need to find the Whale Shark Research Center, and while I'm sure he could tell me where it is, I don't want to go into a whole song and dance about my sister. He seems nice enough, but I'm not interested in bonding with some random guy over our shared grief. I know Pat's still alive. If I'd wanted to waste my time comforting people who think she isn't, I would have stayed home.

Unfortunately, Zach's not easy to dislodge. He trails me off the boat and stands next to me as I look around. There's a bunch of kids who are probably a few years older than me standing on the road just beyond the pier. They shift restlessly, moving around behind some invisible barricade, seeming to jockey for position; and every single one of them is staring at me. I know that sounds new-kid paranoid, but I swear if I had a target on my back and they were snipers, they couldn't be more focused.

"Tell them you're with me," says Zach.

"What?" I cut him a look. Being with him is the last thing I want, though obviously he also senses danger. Maybe they have some weird newcomer hazing ritual here, or maybe they just don't like foreigners, though most of them don't look the least bit Honduran.

"They're from other dive shops," Zach explains. "But I saw you first. I'll get rid of them."

I still don't know what he's talking about, but as I step off the pier I'm swarmed so I have no choice but to follow Zach as he shoves through the crowd, creating a channel for me. He keeps telling people that I'm already signed up, which I don't like the sound of, but it does work. The few people who actually listen to him look disappointed and wander off.

We get to the end of the laneway leading from the pier and pause to look at the town stretching in front of us in three directions. If I keep going straight, the road climbs steeply toward what looks like a mostly residential neighborhood. There are a few motorbikes and pedestrians heading up and down, but it's quiet in comparison to the bustling street running parallel to the ocean. On my right is what looks like a lighthouse, though there's a store on the ground floor with dive equipment in the window. There's another dive shop on my left. And immediately across the road, yet another. I'm relieved to see a bank with an ATM on the fourth corner — at least it's something useful. I'm less thrilled to count three more dive shops without moving from where I'm standing.

"So diving's big here, huh?" I randomly choose a direction and start walking.

"It's the Holy Trinity!" hoots Zach, making devil horns with his fists and punching the air.

"Holy Trinity?" No way am I signing up for some weird religion.

"Diving, drinking and drugs, my man. Everything you could ever need, just the way God intended!"

"Drinking and drugs, huh?" Too bad. It might have been the first religion I could get behind, but the diving's a deal-breaker.

We walk in silence for a couple of minutes. On both sides of the road, there's a single row of one-story shops, a few restaurants and a lot more dive outfits. Most have peeling paint and are losing boards like they've seen one hurricane too many. Flashes of ocean sparkle between the buildings on one side, while the hill backs the buildings on the other. Roads weave up the hill every so often, some paved and some not. None looks wide enough for more than a single car, but since the only vehicles in sight are motorcycles, golf carts and ATVs, I'm guessing that's not a problem. Even this early, the heat is intense.

It takes about two minutes of walking to reach a simple wooden building, much like all the others, with a roughly painted sign that announces it's the Whale Shark Research Center. It was that easy. I stop. Zach stops with me and together we stare at the building. Pat was here less than three weeks ago. She was in that building, talking, laughing and hanging out. I try to picture her here, but I can't. It's not that her ending up in a place like this is a huge surprise. It's exactly the kind of place she dreamed of working in. She has three aquariums at home, all bought with her own money; the biggest cost more than a thousand dollars. She was determined to save the planet, one fish at a time. Maybe I just can't see her here because I don't want to.

A chalkboard out front lists the dates of the most recent whale shark sightings. Did she write on that board? I scan it for her handwriting, but the dates don't go back far enough. The sharks she sighted have been erased. Just like her. I want to shout at someone, demand to know how they can continue with business as usual when my sister is missing.

"That's where she worked," whispers Zach reverently.

I turn to him, startled. For a moment, I'd forgotten he was there. His scrawny body is slumped under the weight of his pack and maybe the weight of a mother who doesn't want him around, not to mention my sister's recent desertion. I debate whether to set him straight on my sister. It's not really his business, but he doesn't strike me as someone who has things go his way very often and I know what that's like.

"She's my sister," I say finally. "Your friend is my sister and she's not dead."

I expect him to demand an explanation, but he just gets very still and his face takes on an expression I recognize all too well. I saw the same expression on my parents' faces when I told them I was going to Utila and bringing Pat home. I hate her for putting me in this position.

ME: *You see what you've done?*

PAT: *You see what you've done.*

ME: *Don't put that on me. You let this guy depend on you. You made him care about you and then you bailed.*

PAT: *You gave him hope.*

"She contacted you?" He interrupts my conversation with Pat, his grin huge.

"Not exactly," I say slowly. I'm wondering where to begin,

but he doesn't wait for details. He just throws his arms around me and pulls me into a fierce hug.

I feel the weight of him and wonder if I made a mistake telling him.

"Cosmic," he hoots, stepping back and holding up his hand for a high five. I slap it and he does a little swaying dance. I smile for the first time in weeks. It's a relief to have someone share my belief that Pat's alive without questioning me. My parents don't count. They want to believe it so badly themselves, I barely had to say a thing to convince them.

"I have to go in there and talk to them." I nod at the Shark Center.

"Right, let's go." He's rocking on the balls of his feet. I think if he wasn't anchored by his pack, he might actually float away.

"I need to do it alone," I say firmly. I don't want to go into a long explanation of how royally I messed up. He doesn't need to know it's my fault Pat came here in the first place. I just hope he'll accept my desire at face value.

He plumps down flat-footed and stares at his feet.

"I'll come find you later," I add quickly. "Where will you be?"

"Bluewater Dive." He's still not looking up. I can tell he thinks I'm blowing him off, so I'm relieved when he continues. "There are rooms behind the dive shack. Anyone can show you. . . ."

"Okay, then. I'll come find you." I want to walk away, but he looks so deflated, I can't make the move. I try to think of something I can say that will bring back his elation of moments before, but I've got nothing.

I wait.

"Right," he says finally, "I guess I better jet."

"We'll meet up later," I promise again. I really wish he would just leave. I'm sorry he's upset, but I can't let him distract me from finding my sister.

We share an awkward silence. I glance back at the Shark Center. He kicks at the sunbaked dirt, stirring up a cloud of dust.

"You'll come round later," he confirms, though it's more question than statement, and he gives me a look at once hopeful and defeated. If there was any part of me doubting whether I'd really make good on my promise, it's squashed in that moment.

"Definitely."

He nods, turns away and plods off down the road, dodging vehicles that are moving too fast and townsfolk barely moving at all. I watch till he's out of sight.

PAT: *You've started something now.*

It's the first time Pat's initiated one of our chats. It catches me off guard and I don't appreciate her tone. I decide to ignore her and go inside the Shark Center. The minute I walk through the door, I remember why I hate Pat's obsession with sea life.

I don't like the ocean. I don't like any natural body of water, not even rivers or lakes. They give me the creeps. The fact is, you never really know what's down there. But oceans are the worst. With oceans, the unknown isn't *what's* down there but *where*. You know there are billions of sharks, eels, octopuses, stingrays, jellyfish, lion fish, sea urchins . . . I could go on. You know that half of what's swimming in the ocean will poison you, maim you or kill you, and you know the other half is just waiting to grow big enough to poison you, maim you or kill you. The only thing you don't know is whether death is a few feet away or a few inches.

The walls of the Whale Shark Research Center are plastered with huge, graphic, high-res close-up photographs of killing machines of every size, shape and description. Or as my sister would say, "marine life."

"You want to swim with the sharks?"

I jump and tear my eyes away from the photographs to stare at the sweet-faced girl with short blond pigtails and soft blue eyes who has just voiced my worst nightmare. She smiles expectantly and comes out from behind a long wooden counter at the far end of the room.

"We get people from all over the world coming just for the chance to spend a few minutes in the water with them. The picture says it all, don't you think?" She stands next to me and we gaze at a four-foot-by-five glossy of a shark whose mouth is twice the length of the full-grown man swimming in front of it.

"It really does," I agree.

"We usually allow only snorkeling with the sharks," she explains in an apologetic voice. "Snorkelers are less stressful for them than divers."

"You certainly wouldn't want to stress them out," I say.

"We have a boat going out this afternoon. I could put your name down for it. All the money from the trips goes into protecting the sharks."

"Protecting the sharks," I repeat.

"It's an experience you'll never forget." She looks up at me with the passionate intensity of a religious zealot.

"I bet."

"It's so amazing," she prattles on. "We go out in the middle of the ocean. From a long way off, we see the seabirds circling this boil of fish — that's what we call it — hundreds of tuna in a frenzy of feeding on smaller fish that are madly eating plankton that the whale sharks have corralled. And we sail right up and dive in the middle of it and —"

"You jump into the middle of the feeding frenzy?" I interrupt.

"Exactly! It's so cool."

"Does anyone ever get bitten in this feeding frenzy?"

"Of course not." She giggles. Nervously.

I give her a skeptical look.

"Almost never."

"Almost never?"

She glances to the back of the shop, where there's an open doorway behind the counter.

"But people do get bitten," I prompt.

"Not by the whale sharks." She folds her arms across her chest and glances back to the door again, like she's willing someone to walk through it.

"But something attacks them."

"The ocean is thousands of feet deep," she says primly. "So obviously there are other things in the water, and if something were to bite, it'd be totally accidental. It could happen anywhere."

"So you're saying that if you jump into thousands of feet of water, in the middle of a feeding frenzy, with little fish and big fish and massive sixty-foot sharks, and everyone's chomping everyone else, it's a total freak accident if something chomps you? It's like walking along the sidewalk and getting swiped by a drunk driver?"

She twists a pigtail around her finger and looks away, frowning.

"I'm looking for Tracy Brandon," I say.

She whips round to stare at me.

"I'm guessing that's you." I try for a friendly smile, which she doesn't return. I don't know what her problem is. She was the one who brought up sharks.

"How can I help you?" she asks grumpily.

"I understand you were my sister's roommate."

"Oh my God!" She puts her hands to her mouth and then clutches my arm. "You're Luke Carrington? Oh, wow, I should have realized. You really look like her. Although you're not much like her, are you?"

"Not much, no." Her reaction doesn't surprise me. Pat's only eleven months older. For years, people mistook us for twins, even teachers who knew Pat was a grade ahead. They just figured I was the dumb one. They weren't far off. Our physical resemblance is striking, and I definitely am the dumb one, if grades are anything to go by.

"I'm so sorry," she says earnestly. "About what happened to her, I mean. Tricia and I were best friends, like sisters almost."

There's that name again. And another best friend? No wonder Pat never had time to call home. In the six weeks she'd been gone before her disappearance, we'd only heard from her twice, and beyond saying she'd been assigned to share a room with this Tracy chick, she didn't say a thing about her. She certainly didn't say they were besties.

"I miss her so much," Tracy says, tearing up. "I can't believe she's gone." One tear slides down her cheek, followed by another.

"I was hoping I could ask you some questions," I say, keeping my voice calm. Now I'm the one looking at the door. I know where this is going. After my parents came back with the police report and before I decided to fetch Pat home myself, I spent almost a week with sobbing females; every relative, friend, teacher, random stranger that could claim some connection to my perfect sister turned up in our living room doing exactly what this girl is about to do. She shudders once — and so it begins — throws her arms around my neck and starts heaving loud wet sobs. I put an arm around her, pat her back and wonder if I can ease off my backpack without her noticing. The three flights, two-hour bus ride and life-threatening ocean crossing are catching up with me. Leading her over to a corner set up like a reading nook, I ease her down into a chair. Unfortunately, she doesn't loosen her death grip on my neck. I use my foot to pull over another chair for myself and sink down with her.

I want to comfort her, but something — I'm not sure what — stops me from sharing my conviction that Pat's still alive. As unlikely a soulmate as Zach may have been for my sister, I can see her taking him under her wing. But this girl, with her bland prettiness and ability to switch from chirpy to pitiful in under a minute, doesn't seem like someone Pat would ever befriend.

"It's going to be okay," I say, rubbing Tracy's back, which is sticky with sweat. Of course, there's no AC, even though it's a hundred degrees in here. They wouldn't want to divert money from protecting the sixty-foot predators.

She sniffles and rubs her face against my chest. I'm pretty sure she just rubbed snot on my shirt, but when she looks up, I'm so relieved to see the fountain is running dry that I give her an encouraging smile. She heaves one last raggedy breath and finally loosens her grip. I drop my arm and gently pull away from her to stand up beside my chair. If there's one thing I know about crying females, it's that it's not over till it's over, so I don't walk away just yet.

"I'm sorry," she says. "I should be the one comforting you."

"No," I say quickly and glance at the door again. "I'm good." Is there no one else staffing this damn place?

"You're so nice." She stands up and steps toward me. I back up an equal distance and bump into the wall. The shop seems to have shrunk.

"Would you like to see my room?" Her pink skin turns three shades darker. "I mean Tricia's room?"

"Maybe later." I take a couple of casual sideways steps along the wall until she's no longer between me and the exit. "I really just wanted to ask if there's anything you could tell me about her."

"There's so much I could tell you." Her eyes start filling again.

"Maybe when you're feeling better," I say over my shoulder, as I make a break for the door I came in.

"I'd love to talk to you about her." She's right behind me. I speed up.

"G'day, shark lover!" We're both halted in our tracks by a cheerful voice reverberating off the walls. A stocky, completely bald giant chooses this moment, when I'm less than a yard from freedom, to swagger out from the back door and hustle over to plant himself between me and the exit.

"Have ya signed up for a trip, mate?" he grins, showing a mouthful of strong white teeth in a tanned, leathery face. I get from the accent that he's Australian. Zach was right about Utila being a hodgepodge of nationalities. I figure Tracy for American.

"Dr. Jake," says Tracy, moving to stand beside him, "this is Luke, Tricia's brother."

"Ah, I see." He holds out a hand, which I take, and he claps his other hand on my shoulder. "We were all very fond of your sister. It was a bad business, that. I gave your parents the report we got from the police. It seemed pretty cut-and-dried, I'm afraid. They found her clothes on a dock on the outskirts of town. We figure she'd gone out swimming a bit too deep and an undertow took her. She'd been drinking as well, you see." The bluster that filled him moments before has leaked out, but the hand that grips my shoulder is firm. "I'm sorry, son." He gives my shoulder a squeeze.

I remember it was this man who sent the first e-mail when Pat didn't show up for work. At that point, she'd been missing less than twelve hours. My parents made a show of scoffing at the childless man who was so quick to worry about one missed shift.

"Imagine if we worried every time you stayed out all night and missed a day of school?" said Dad, but his brow furrowed exactly the way it does every time I stay out all night and miss school. My dad talks a good game, but if anyone knows bad things happen to good people, he does.

Two days later, this man wrote again. He'd been to the police, but they said it was too early to investigate.

"Of course it is," Mom snapped, knocking back her Chardonnay and refilling her glass. "She probably just met someone and is having a bit of fun."

She didn't say anything more, but it was obvious she was scared. Not because she was drinking — it's rare Mom doesn't have a drink in her hand — but we all knew Pat wasn't the kind of girl to disappear with some random guy. She herself was the product of Mom's bit of fun in eleventh grade. By the time Pat had incubated for nine months on a steady diet of nachos and wine spritzers, she'd had all the fun she could take.

The third e-mail confirmed Pat officially missing, but by then Mom had already gotten me booking their flights on the Internet. I would have gone with them, but we were borrowing cash from Mom's parents for their tickets and Pat hates it when we accept anything from the grandparents. It just gives them one more excuse to remind Mom she threw her life away when she got pregnant and married Dad.

I was sure they'd find Pat and the whole thing would turn out to be some crazy misunderstanding. Maybe she'd gone over to the mainland for a couple of days and left word with someone who forgot to pass on the message to her boss. Having now met her roommate, Tracy, I could definitely see her doing something like that. It wasn't until my parents returned after only forty-eight hours, with nothing but resignation and an obviously bogus police report, that I realized there was something seriously wrong and I'd have to go after Pat myself. It took all my summer earnings and another loan from Mom's parents, but I don't even care if Pat gets pissed this time. It's not like she's left me any choice. She's either in trouble or being a total flake. Either way, I need to find her.

I draw in a shaky breath and force myself to look Dr. Jake in the eye. "We appreciate all your help, sir," I say politely, though a million questions crowd my brain. How could anyone who knew my sister really believe she could get swept away by a rogue current, so intoxicated she couldn't swim? Even if she *has* started drinking, and I still doubt that, Pat has as much chance of death by drowning as the whale sharks she's so in love with. I'd really like to know how this man could spend so much time with my sister and not understand the first thing about her. I remind myself that he's only trying to help. And it doesn't matter what he thinks, anyway. I'm here now, and I'm not leaving without my sister.

CHAPTER 3

I'm in a small, sparsely furnished room with two single beds and a wooden desk. Dr. Jake insisted I stay in one of the dozen or so identical rooms behind the shop that are used by research interns and backpackers, who aren't satisfied risking their lives once in shark-infested waters but want to stay on and do it repeatedly. He wouldn't let me pay. I didn't argue because I'm short on cash and who knows how long I'll need to survive here while I search for my sister. He even said I should come to him if I need anything else. He said it like he meant it, and it occurred to me it's the first time in my life anyone's ever made me an offer like that. Of course, my parents would do anything for me if they could, but drinking takes up a lot of Mom's time and looking after her takes up most of Dad's.

I'm lying on one of the beds, the contents of my pack strewn on the other. The ceiling fan is pushing sweltering air around the room without providing any relief, but I find the predictability of its steadily rotating wings comforting. I'm not sure how long I've been staring up at it. I need a shower. Dr. Jake pointed out the communal washrooms when he showed me to the room. He even gave me a towel and plastic flip-flops. I know I need to get back to work investigating Pat's disappearance, but I feel like I'm glued to this bed. I never thought it would be this hard.

ME: *You should have warned me.*

PAT: *About what?*

ME: *These people. All of them mourning you, like you're actually dead. How many more are there? Am I going to keep tripping over them like landmines?*

PAT: *Is that what you're really worried about? Or are you starting to wonder if they might be right about me?*

ME:

I stand up, slide on the flip-flops, grab the towel and slam the door on my way out, not bothering to lock it. I don't own anything worth stealing.

There's no hot water in the shower, but it feels good to let the cool water run down my body, washing away the grime of the last twenty-four hours. I raise my face into the stream and start as I notice a freaking huge tarantula just above the showerhead. Drops of water glisten on its hairy body. I wonder if this is why Dr. Jake gave me the flip-flops. I take one off and raise it threateningly, but the spider doesn't budge. I sigh, turn off the shower, quickly dry off and wrap the towel around my waist. Opening the door onto the narrow paved walkway that leads to the rooms in one direction and to the sea in the other, I don't have to look far before I come across a plastic pail. It takes longer to find something flat, and I finally go back to my room for a piece of paper. Ready for business, I return to find the spider has advanced down the wall like he was coming to find me.

"You have to understand, buddy, it's nothing personal. It's just that you're butt-ugly and I can't leave you here for some girl to find. Most girls are irrational when it comes to spiders. I'm doing you a favor. Trust me."

I cover him with the pail and slide the paper underneath. I flip it fast, expecting him to drop to the bottom, but he clings to the paper so I feel his body, larger than my hand, clinging to the other side. I step out of the shower and gently jiggle him as I take a few steps down the path, walking away from the rooms. He continues hanging on to the paper, but seems calm as he waits for my next move.

"You've done this before, haven't you, Spidey?"

"What you got there?" I jump and almost drop the pail as a girl about my own age steps out of the next washroom with a cleaning brush in her hand. Her black hair is woven tightly to her head, finishing in short braids that peter out to nothing, like they've given up. But the light in her dark eyes is compelling, as if there's a whole long story unfolding behind them.

"What you doing with my bucket?" she demands.

"Nothing," I say.

She raises an eyebrow. "You got something in that bucket?"

I think about that for a moment. I've already made one girl cry today and while something tells me it would take a lot to make this one break down, there's only so much crying a guy can take in one day. I've reached my limit.

"A frog," I say, looking at her steadily.

"Let me see," she says. "I'm from the island. Maybe I can tell you what kinda frog you got." She glances at the bucket, then back at me.

"I'm sorry, I can't do that." I pause. "It's a poison frog."

"A poison frog?" She gives me a hard look, then bites her lip as if she's struggling not to smile.

"Yes, there are many poison frogs in Central America. You're a native. You should know that."

"I've never seen a poison frog on Utila."

"Have you ever seen a huge hairy tarantula on Utila?"

"Well, yes, as a matter o' fact I have, and I can't say I'm partial to 'em."

"Exactly. Now if you'll just step aside, I need to take my poison frog for a little walk. Do you have any suggestions where he might like to go?"

"Down the toilet," she says flatly. "And flush 'im twice."

"Thank you for your suggestion, but my poison frog would rather return to his natural habitat."

"Then you need to turn yourself around and go straight on outta here." She points with her cleaning brush for emphasis. "You're heading to the dock. You need to take him in the other direction, turn either way when you get to the road, take the first turn and head up the hill, walk for ten minutes till you get past all the houses. Then you'll come to some pastures; keep walking another five minutes till you get to the forest. I expect your poison frog will be very happy there."

"Perhaps it has escaped your attention that I'm only wearing a towel and flip-flops."

"Good thing you got your flip-flops. That road gets rough."

I try to stare her down, but she meets my glare with a determined one of her own. My best bet is to take him in the direction of the dock behind her. There's a spindly tree at the edge of the seawall. I could put him on it. Spidey shifts restlessly under my hand. He's been upside down for a while now. All the blood is probably rushing to his spidey-head.

"So you gonna hand over that ugly thing or what?" Setting down the cleaning brush, she puts out her hands and beckons impatiently.

"You want my poison frog?" I'm certain I've misunderstood.

"No, I want your ugly-ass spider. Gah, I hate those things!"

"What are you going to do with him?"

"I'm gonna throw him a party," she snaps. "The Good Lord was taking a nap when you were born, wasn't He? Give it here." She steps closer and snatches the pail out of my hands. "Damn tourists," she mutters as she pushes past me and stomps down the path, past the rooms, to the front of the property. It's a short walk. She passes under the entrance arch, with its crumbling cement and exposed iron rods, and disappears around the corner.

I hesitate for a moment, wondering if I should follow her. She's probably going to kill him the second she's out of sight, but Pat's the animal lover, not me. I don't suppose one less tarantula is going to do anyone any harm.

Back in my room, I throw on some clothes and head out to the shop to look for Tracy and Dr. Jake. I still haven't questioned either of them about my sister. I enter through the back, which is an office behind the shop, and emerge from the door that Tracy and I were staring at this morning. I find her sitting behind the counter, chatting with a guy I haven't met. Dr. Jake is nowhere in sight.

"Luke!" Tracy exclaims. She hops off her stool and rushes over to grab my arm and drag me along to the other guy.

"This is Pete," she says. She doesn't say who I am.

"Hey, man." Pete holds out a hand for me to shake, which I do. "We're all really sorry about your sister. Tricia was a great girl, and smart. I thought for sure she'd be running this place someday. She had a real affinity with the fish, like she could see inside their heads. You know?"

"Yeah, I know. I always wished I had fins and a tail."

Pete chuckles.

I try to look like I'm joking, but it's so not a joke I don't know where to begin.

"So I was wondering what you guys could tell me about her last days. Was she acting strange at all?"

Pete and Tracy exchange looks. The silence extends beyond awkward.

"What?" I prompt.

"Well, you know your sister." Pete smiles, glances at Tracy and stops.

"Yeah, I know my sister." I'm starting to feel annoyed. "What about her?"

"Well, she was kind of wild, man. No offense or anything."

"She wasn't a skank," Tracy interjects.

I turn to stare at her.

"No, not a skank, really," Pete agrees slowly.

"What the hell are you two talking about?" I demand. "*Who* are you talking about?"

They exchange looks again. I'm not much of a brawler, but I size up Fishboy for the first time. I could easily take him. I cross my arms over my chest.

"I don't know what you're implying, but my sister does not sleep around." I struggle to keep my voice even.

Tracy takes a sudden interest in a thread that's come loose on her T-shirt.

"Maybe you should talk to her boyfriend," Pete says.

"Mark?" This is the weirdest conversation I've had about my sister yet.

Tracy snaps to attention. "Who's Mark?"

"Her boyfriend since eighth grade, but she broke up with him before she came down here." I want to add "What's it to you?" because she seems way too interested and is now sending so many messages to Fishboy with her raised brows and rolling eyes that they might as well be tapping out Morse code.

"Jamie," says Pete.

"Who?" I ask.

"She was going out with a local boy, Jamie Greenfield."

"So she's a skank because she had one boyfriend?" I choose to ignore the sting that Pat didn't bother to mention her new boyfriend. Things were a little strained between us just before she left home, but Pat and I have always been close. Having messed-up parents will do that for you.

"Well, he was the most recent," Tracy explains carefully and steps away from me when I whip round to glare at her.

"Look, maybe we're wrong." Pete holds up both palms. "You should talk to Jamie. But Tricia was a pretty girl, and she always had a ton of guys hanging around her. That's all we're saying. . . ."

He turns to Tracy for confirmation and she gives a small nod.

"Where does Jamie live?" I demand.

"It's a blue house up the hill from the fire station. Just ask for Miss Bertie — she's his grandmother. Any local can direct you. But there's no point going until this evening. He works pretty much 24/7, and he's a carpenter so he's all over the island and the little cays. He won't be home much before seven or eight."

"Thanks," I say more politely than I'm feeling and stalk out to the street. These two are so far off base about my sister, it's laughable.

I check my watch and realize I have a few hours to kill while I wait for Pat's boyfriend to come home. I could walk around seeing who else on this island knew her, but it's been a long day and I have a sudden and overpowering need to get high. I know it's the last thing I should be thinking about at a time like this, but Pat's the responsible one in our family, not me. She took care of all of us, even more than Dad, sweet guy though he is. He's a photographer, so he doesn't make great money and often has to work long hours, which left Pat making sure dinner got made and Mom's car keys were hidden when she'd had too much to drink, which was practically every night. Pat held it all together and was surprisingly good at making it all look easy.

I knew, though. Always having to be vigilant cost her, and sooner or later something was bound to go drastically wrong. The cracks were beginning to show, even before Mom did what she did and Pat took off to Honduras. I wasn't expecting Pat to completely disappear off the radar, but for ages I'd been anticipating disaster, like a Mayan awaiting the apocalypse. Maybe that's why I like to get high. When I'm stoned is about the only time I don't feel scared. And right now, in this moment, when everything I hear about my sister makes her sound like a stranger and no one can tell me where she is, the fear is suffocating.

I just need a couple of hours of peace. But where am I going to score weed on an island where I don't know a soul?

And then it comes to me.

Zach.

CHAPTER 4

"ude, are you sure they said Miss Bertie's house?"

I slow down for a minute to tug on Zach, who's stalled again in the middle of the road. We've passed out of the main part of town. It's dark, with no streetlights, and the houses, crouching in overgrown yards, are dimly lit or shuttered and empty. Massive trees, with thick leafy branches and hanging vines, cast shadows that seem to move with a life of their own. Bats swoop overhead, and the occasional scuttling noises make us both jump; but something else, beyond the obvious creep factor, is freaking Zach out. He did try to explain when we were a few hours into the weed, but I couldn't follow his logic then, and now I'm no longer interested. We're going to find Miss Bertie's house. End of story.

I stop in front of a white picket fence. I can see a blue wooden house behind it. These are the only two clues we have, beyond rambling directions from various locals. I look to Zach for confirmation.

"You said you'd know it when you see it, Zach. Is this it or not?"

"Oh, man." He wraps his arms around his body and leans over like he's going to puke.

"If you're going to do it, buddy, now's the time. Once we go through this gate, you're just going to have to hold it in. Do you hear what I'm saying?"

He nods but doesn't straighten up, so I lean on the gate and wait.

"That your gate?" a familiar voice bellows from the porch. "I'm thinking it must be, the way you're lounging all over it."

Since the fence is only four feet tall, I can comfortably look over to see who's shouting, but I don't need to. I lean forward and give Zach a jab in the ribs. "You could have warned me, man!"

"Reesie Greenfield lives here," he whispers.

"Yeah? Thanks."

I turn around, grateful it's too dark for her to see my eyes, which are most likely bloodshot.

"Excuse me, miss." I hope to God I'm not slurring my words. "I was wondering if Jamie Greenfield happened to be at home."

"Well, I don't know. He might be out hunting poison frogs. You know, we've got an invasion of 'em here on the island."

I swing open the gate, march through and walk up her sand path until I'm right under where she's standing on her broken-down porch. I look up into bottomless brown eyes.

"How fortunate we have you to help in their safe relocation."

"My brother's not here. What d'you want him for?"

Without waiting for an answer, she leans on the porch railing and hollers out to the street again. "That you out there, Zach O'Donell?"

Zach makes a strangled noise that's hard to interpret. I turn to see that he's standing upright now but staying well back from the gate.

"You bringing your stupid-ass drugs to my house?" demands Reesie.

Zach shakes his head, which would be hard to see in the darkness except that he throws his whole body into it, twisting vigorously from side to side.

"That boy is crazy," Reesie mutters before bawling at him again. "You better stop lurking around out there or someone's gonna think you're a thief and take a shot at you!"

Zach doesn't move.

"Get on in here!"

Zach walks slowly forward, opens the gate, lets himself into the yard and stops.

"Right here," says Reesie, pointing to the empty air beside me. "I want to get a good look at you. Last time I saw you, you were lying in your own puke. Nice to see you up and around."

"Cosmic," says Zach, but you can tell he doesn't mean it.

"Poison-frog boy and the pothead. Should have known you two would find each other." She says it under her breath but loud enough for us to hear. "So you gonna introduce me to your new friend, Zach?"

"Luke, this is Reesie," says Zach miserably. "She doesn't like me," he whispers.

"Not like you?" Reesie snorts. "Why would I not like you? I just love cleaning up puke. And when you miss the toilet and piss on the bathroom floor, I feel like opening a bottle of champagne, 'cause I get to clean that up, too."

"Reesie works at Bluewater," Zach explains, staring at his feet.

I wonder how old she is. Cleaning the dive hotels seems like a crappy job for a kid. No pun intended.

I give Zach a pat on the shoulder and try to steer the conversation back to the point. "We were hoping to speak to your brother."

"Why?" She crosses her arms and gives me a hard look.

I debate telling her it's none of her business, but it doesn't seem worth the fight.

"I want to ask him about my sister."

"Who's your sister?"

"Patricia Carrington, the girl who disappeared."

"I knew her," she says in a softer tone, uncrossing her arms. "But I don't know why you'd be wanting to speak to Jamie about her. I don't believe he ever met her."

I clear my throat. "I heard they were dating."

"No," says Reesie. "My brother knows better than to go out with crazy tourists."

"Crazy?" I snap. "How well did you know my sister?"

"Look, I heard she drowned, and I'm really sorry about that. She seemed like a nice girl, but the tourist kids who come here are out of control, you know? I don't know how they behave back home, but when they come here, they act like what they do doesn't count. There's some local boys will take advantage of that. But my brother's not one of them."

We all look over as we hear the gate open behind us. A tall thin guy steps into the porch light and walks up to where we're standing. He wearily rubs a hand across his eyes but smiles warmly at Zach.

"Hey, Zach," he says, holding out his fist. Zach bangs it with his own and grins.

"This is Jamie," Zach says, standing a little taller.

"What you boys be doing my way?" asks Jamie, looking at me intently.

"I wanted to ask you about my sister, Patricia."

Jamie nods his head, like I've just solved a puzzle. "You take after her."

"You knew her?" exclaims Reesie. "How'd you manage that? You hardly ever came around the Shark Center."

Jamie looks past me to Zach, then glances at his sister. "I knew her," he affirms softly, before leaning down to where a piece of siding has come loose under the porch. He reaches into his tool belt for his hammer and steadies the board as he taps the nail back in.

I turn to Zach, but he's taking a sudden interest in the stars, gazing skyward like he's expecting a celestial event.

"Were you going out with her?" I demand, turning back to Jamie.

"I already told you he wasn't," Reesie answers for him, but doubt has crept into her voice.

Jamie stands up slowly, turning his back to his sister. "I know how hard this must be for you," he says. "Trish was . . ." He hesitates, as if searching for the right word or the courage to say it, but in the end just crouches back down to the siding, pulling at another loose board. He wiggles it into place as Reesie tracks his every move.

"You best get on home," she says finally. "We really are sorry for your loss."

We all watch Jamie bang in another nail. There's not a wasted movement as he methodically takes the broken pieces of his home and makes it whole.

"Well, if you think of anything . . ." I say.

Jamie stands up and steps toward me, meeting my eyes with a steady gaze. "I'm glad you came by, Luke. It was nice to meet you. I really wish there was something I could do." He puts out his hand, taking mine and holding it for a moment. His hand is roughly callused yet weirdly comforting. I let go first.

"Drop around anytime," Jamie calls out as we reach the gate. I turn to respond, but he's already disappearing into his house. Reesie's still on the porch, though, staring down at the siding that her brother was working on, lost in thought.

Zach and I walk down the hill in silence. There was something going on back there, but I don't know if it had anything to do with Pat. It's been a long day, and I can't think straight — may have to lay off the drugs for a while.

"Do you think they were lying?" I ask. We're close enough to the main street now to hear music blaring from the bars, and a few streetlights make the potholed road less treacherous. We speed up a little.

"Jamie's solid," says Zach.

"Yeah, but do you think Jamie was dating my sister?"

Zach exhales loudly. "He was with Tricia a lot, man, pretty much since she first arrived. That's mostly how I know him, but he always said we couldn't tell Reesie."

I stop abruptly and turn to him. "Why didn't you say anything before?" I demand.

Zach kicks a rotting mango to the other side of the road. I suddenly notice the air is rank with the smell of rotting fruit. It seems to be dropping off the trees faster than people can pick it. Zach takes off his flip-flop and examines mango chunks that have lodged in the strap. He tries to shake them off, but they're stuck fast. Dropping down on one knee, he rubs his flip-flop against the pavement.

"You're scared of Reesie?" I ask, though I know the answer.

Zach continues working away at the fruit, but he nods his head.

"It's okay, man," I say. I can feel the beginning of a headache pulsing behind my eyes. I press my fingers into my forehead and massage my temples. "I'll sort it out tomorrow."

He looks up at me, the streetlight skimming off his face like a halo. "You're not angry?"

"You kidding?" I grin, shoving down my frustration. "That girl would spook a fully armed marine on steroids."

Zach jumps up and throws his arms around me, his slimy sandal whacking me on the back.

I give him a one-armed hug before shoving him back and holding him firm so I can look him in the eye. "But you tell me everything from here on in. Right, buddy?"

"Brother from another mother!" crows Zach, holding out his hand for me to slap. He follows this with a complicated ritual of finger snapping, fist banging and more palm slapping, which he has to teach me because I didn't grow up on a hippie commune in the sixties. I am *so* in over my head with this guy.

We amble on down to the junction at the bottom of the hill. The pier is straight ahead, and lights from fishing boats twinkle just beyond. If you didn't know we were surrounded by billions of cubic feet of water, harboring every monster known to man and some we haven't even discovered yet, it would be almost pretty. Music from a nearby bar is deafening, but it doesn't drown out the occasional hoots from drunken patrons.

"Go for a beer?" asks Zach hopefully.

"Sorry, dude, I'm wiped."

"It's okay. See ya on the flip side." He gives a little salute and heads into the nearest bar.

I try not to think about how I'm no closer to finding Pat as I trudge back to the Shark Center. Instead, I think about the last time I saw her. I'd refused to see her off at the airport when she left for Utila. I wanted her to think I was angry. I should have known Pat would never leave it at that. She came down to the basement, where I was hunched over on the sofa rolling a joint, a half-finished beer on the table beside me. Normally, seeing me like that would have earned me a twenty-minute tirade on my wasted potential. But Pat was in a hurry. She tousled my hair, something she hadn't done in a long time.

"So, are you going to miss me, little brother?" she teased. I allowed myself a moment of satisfaction that she sounded happy, happier than she'd been in weeks.

She waited for me to reply, but I wouldn't look at her. I couldn't. I knew she'd see in my face how much I wanted her to stay. I carefully tucked in a few stray leaves that were trailing out one side of the joint, licked the paper and twisted the ends into maybe the tidiest reefer I'd ever rolled. Taking out my lighter, I lit up, pulling the first hit into my lungs so slowly, I could feel every sensation as it whispered through my body. Only when the sound of her receding footsteps disappeared did I sneak a glance. Her back was rigid, her steps brisk as she walked toward the stairs. She hesitated for a moment, maybe waiting for me to call out to her. But I kept silent, and she didn't look back as she took the stairs two at a time.

I crossed the room and stood in the spot she'd so recently vacated, listening to her and my parents moving around, carrying the last of her bags out to the car. A couple of times she passed the open doorway to the basement and I had to scuttle backwards, scared she'd catch me lurking. I was sure she'd come back to say good-bye, even if it was just a shout down the stairs. Only when I heard the front door slam did I realize she was gone. I tore up the stairs and went straight to the living room window. As the car turned out of the driveway, I caught a glimpse of her, but she was facing forward. That was Pat, always more interested in where she was going than in what was she was leaving behind. I didn't blame her. I didn't blame her one bit.

Bats frolic in the lamplight, swooping close to my head as they dive for the mosquitoes feasting on my flesh. Music and laughter waft out of the bars, and I'm slowed down by multiple invitations from total strangers to get hammered or stoned. I wonder how many of these people knew my sister. I admit the idea of getting wrecked again is tempting, but the pulsing behind my eyes has turned into a wicked throbbing and I'm starting to worry the weed I smoked earlier was cut with something more lethal than the usual shit. By the time I reach my room, all I'm thinking about is a cold shower and bed, so when I see my front step occupied, I seriously consider walking right by.

"Luke," she says, getting to her feet.

"Tracy," I say.

I don't ask her what the hell she's doing on my doorstep, but I'm pretty sure she hears it in my voice.

"I want to apologize," she says quickly, "for what Pete and I said earlier."

I don't say anything.

"I know what you must have thought this morning, how you must have felt. . . ."

No, you really don't.

"I mean, I can't imagine how awful this must be for you. . . ." Her eyes start welling up.

"It's okay," I say quickly, hoping to avoid a repeat of this morning's performance.

No such luck. She heaves a big one, and the waterworks resume.

I sigh, which she takes as some kind of invitation to leap into my arms.

Again.

"Do you want to come inside?" I ask, because my own legs are about to give out and I'm stupid enough to think I can get rid of her if I calm her down.

She nods her head, now buried in my chest, so I awkwardly shuffle her backwards into my room.

I look around for a tissue. Of course I don't have any, though the way things have been going lately, I should really get some. I ease her down onto my bed and slump next to her as wetness seeps through my shirt.

"I miss Tricia so much," she blubbers.

"I know." As uncharitable as it is, given this girl's obvious grief at losing my sister, I still wonder how they could have been friends. They couldn't be more different. Pat and I have been through some heavy crap in our lives, and I've never seen Pat cry — not once. She's probably a little too stoic, but that's the kind of person she admires as well. She has no patience for crybabies.

"Can you forgive me?" She looks into my eyes with her huge blue saucers.

"Absolutely," I say. If we can wrap this up quickly, I might still get a shower.

She releases my neck and lies down on my bed.

"Tracy," I say firmly. "You can't stay here."

She sits up again.

And takes off her shirt.

"Tracy." I'm a little less firm this time. At least my voice is. "You really need to go."

She puts one hand behind her back and in a fluid move-ment, like a magician or a porn star, she makes her bra disappear. I look down at it on the floor and I don't know how it got there. She lies back on my bed and wriggles out of her shorts. No underwear. Of course.

And no bikini line.

And sun-bleached hair and a rockin' body.

Uh-oh.

Me: *I think your friend's coming on to me.*

Pat: *What was your first clue, Sherlock?*

Sitting up again, Tracy grabs the edge of my shirt, flipping it over my head and off.

I could have stopped her. I'm twice her size.

ME: *What should I do?*

PAT: *Not inviting her into your bedroom would have been a good start.*

Tracy starts stroking my leg.

PAT: *Snap out of it, Luke! You can't go along with this.*

ME: *It's really none of your business.*

PAT: *But she's needy and emotional. That's not even your type.*

ME: *She's naked and willing. That's every guy's type.*

Tracy's hand migrates to the waistband of my shorts. Suddenly my fly's undone. Like magic. The girl is skillful.

PAT: *She called me a skank.*

ME: *Technically, she said you weren't a skank.*

"Lie down, Luke, I'm so lonely. I just need you to hold me."

PAT: *You know this isn't right.*

"Goddamnit," I mutter, as I button my shorts. It doesn't help that I agree with her. Tracy really isn't my type, and even if she was, I could never get past what she said about Pat. But just once I'd like to do something wrong without Pat's voice in my head telling me not to — and I don't mean just since her disappearance. I didn't used to actually hear her voice like I do now, but I've felt it, like a goody-two-shoes soundtrack always playing in the background. Even booze doesn't drown her out. Believe me, I've tried.

"Tracy," I begin . . .

We both flinch, as there's a rap on the door.

I get up to answer it.

"Ignore it, baby," coos crazy naked girl.

I dive for the door. I don't care who it is. Anyone is a welcome distraction right now.

Okay, I was wrong.

I gape at Reesie, standing on my doorstep.

"Who you got in there?" she demands.

"Who are you, my mother?"

"Don't you insult your mama to me, boy. I bet she's thinking you're safe asleep in your bed right now. What's she gonna think if she knows what you're really up to?"

"Knowing my mom, she'd be thinking, *Rock on*."

"How long you been on this island?"

She doesn't wait for me to answer.

"You've not been here twenty-four hours and already you've got a girl in your bed. Haven't you ever heard of sexually transmitted diseases? You're just like all the rest. You don't even know that girl. You can't know that girl. You haven't been here long enough. You just —"

"REESIE!"

We both jump, and I notice for the first time that Jamie is standing behind his sister.

"Don't you shout at me, Jamie Greenfield. Not after what you've been up to. You're no better than him. Why, you two should form your own club, Randy-ass Boys of Utila."

Jamie peers around his sister and catches my eye.

"Well, go on then," Reesie says, glaring at Jamie. "Go ahead and tell him the truth this time. That's what we came here for." She crosses her arms and taps her foot like she's marking out time.

"I'm sorry," says Jamie, his shoulders drooping on his

lanky frame, his dark eyes deep wells of pain. "I just didn't see the point in bringing it all up. I know Trish didn't tell you about me. Maybe she had her reasons." He cuts a look at Reesie. "I guess we were both trying to keep it low-key till we figured out where we were headed."

"You mean you were lying to my face," says Reesie.

Jamie gives her a guilty look before turning back to me. "This sure isn't how I hoped we'd first meet," he sighs, "but I loved your sister, Luke, and she loved me."

"What?" I stare at him stupidly.

"We were gonna get married," he continues.

"But we never even heard of you," I exclaim. "You couldn't have known her more than five or six weeks."

"Oh, that's perfect," hoots Reesie. "You're gonna give him advice on not rushing relationships."

"I don't know what happened to her," says Jamie, ignoring his sister. "Drowning seems like the last thing that could happen, but they found her clothes on the dock, and I haven't seen her since, and I know she wouldn't disappear on purpose. She was making a life here."

"Come back to bed, baby," calls Tracy.

Reesie raises an eyebrow.

"Look," I say. "I want to finish this conversation, but I'm kind of busy right now."

"Oh, we can see you're busy," says Reesie.

"I'm really sorry, Luke," says Jamie. It's not clear whether he's apologizing for his sister or mine, but I'm relieved when he drags Reesie off the stoop. Of course, this incites her to new levels of outrage. She keeps up a steady rant as he drags her down the path.

I rub the back of my neck before going inside. Tracy is under the sheet, which happens to be the only covering on the bed. She raises one corner invitingly and grins, but her confidence wavers when I glare at her and don't move from the open doorway.

"You have to go."

She waits a few beats, then finally leans over the bed and grabs her clothes, pulling them on under the sheet. She doesn't say anything as she stalks past me. I'm just about to close the door when she gasps and drops to her knees. I think maybe it's a trick to get back inside, but she's reaching under the stoop, clearly after something other than me.

"I can't reach it," she says. "Help me."

I come outside and kneel on the wooden step, looking through the opening in the slats to the thing Tracy is grop- ing for. She moves aside and I take her place, feeling around underneath the steps till my hand hits soft fabric. I grab it and pull it out, turning it over in my hand. It's a small, roughly stitched cloth doll with what looks like human hair glued to its head, straight black hair like mine — or my sister's.

"What is it?" I ask, glancing at Tracy, but the look on her face is enough to tell me I don't want to know.

"Tricia found one of these the day before she went miss- ing," she whispers.

I don't know who she thinks might be listening, but I'm more annoyed than scared. It's late, I'm bone-tired, I've just learned my sister had not just a secret boyfriend but a secret fiancé, some ravenous, invisible insects are biting every inch of my exposed torso and I've had enough of this girl.

I sink down on the top step, lean my head on the newel post and wait for her to continue because I know nothing short of a heart attack is going to stop her. She settles on the step below me.

"It's a voodoo doll," she explains. "Some of the locals here, the Garifuna, practice the old religions brought over from Africa."

"Garifuna?"

"African descendants, like Reesie and her brother."

"Don't you mean Caribbean?"

"Yes, but where do you think the Caribbean people came from?"

"I thought voodoo came from Haiti."

"That's just one form of it."

"You seem very well-informed."

"Of course. I looked into it after what happened to Tricia."

"So, let me get this straight," I say slowly, though at this point my own mind's so muddy, I'm not sure I'm capable of rational thought. "You're trying to tell me Reesie and my sister's boyfriend were practicing voodoo and did something to her?"

She shrugs and stands up. "Believe what you want," she says, in a wounded voice. "All I'm saying is that a lot of the locals still practice the black arts, and Tricia found a doll like this under her step the day before she went missing."

So much tension courses out of my body when I see her turn away and start down the path to her own room that I almost fall off the step. She stops when she gets to her door and turns back to me. Her face is completely hidden in the shadows, but her disembodied voice rings out, piercing the stillness of the night. "Be careful who you make friends with," she warns.

As she disappears into her room, goose bumps ripple across my flesh. I go inside, but despite my exhaustion, it's a long time before I fall asleep.

CHAPTER 5

I go looking for Zach first thing the next morning. I want to pump him for information on this voodoo crap before hunting down Jamie to see what else he knows about Pat. I don't get as far as Bluewater before Zach hails me from the front porch of a restaurant. I guess that's an advantage of only one main street — you're never too far from every other person you've ever met.

I climb the rickety wooden stairs and join him on the veranda overlooking the street. Despite the early hour, I'm surprised to see quite a few other young people, most sporting rumpled beachwear, already tucking into hearty breakfasts. Everyone seems to be eating variations of rice and beans, which doesn't appeal to me at this time of day, but I'm cheered to discover Zach with a traditional American breakfast. My stomach rumbles as I flop down in the chair opposite him, take a piece of toast off his plate and munch it thoughtfully.

"How's it going?" I ask.

"I have to get someone to sign up for a dive," he says glumly, spearing a piece of egg and shoveling it into his mouth.

"Your boss still on your ass?"

He nods.

"Do you know anything about voodoo?" He perks up at the change of subject and leans back in his chair.

"You've come to the right place, my brother." He grins. "What do you want to know?"

A waiter comes over and I order eggs, bacon, the whole nine yards. I have a feeling it's going to be a long day. When he's gone, I pull the doll out of my pocket and set it on the table. It's a bit crushed and some of the hair has fallen off. Its mouth is a jagged line of red cross-stitching, with single black cross-stitches for each eye. Is it possible for a doll to look dead?

Zach's eyes grow big as he backs his chair away from the table. "Where'd you get that?" he squeaks, keeping his eye on the doll.

"Stay cool, buddy. It's not going to bite you."

"Oh man, oh man." Zach's voice rises hysterically. I look around to see if we're attracting attention and notice for the first time that most of the patrons look either hungover or half-asleep. "Where'd it come from?"

"I found it under my front step."

Zach leaps to his feet, knocking over his chair. "We've got to get rid of it," he says urgently.

He looks like he means right now, but I just ordered breakfast and I'm not going anywhere without some fuel.

"Sit down, Zach," I say firmly, taking the doll off the table and shoving it back in my pocket. He stares at me like I'm crazy, but he rights his chair and sits down, keeping well back from the table. And me.

"This is bad," he says. "This is very, very bad."

"So you do know what it is?"

"Don't you?" he demands, keeping his eye on the pocket where I shoved the doll.

"Tracy said it's a voodoo doll. She said Pat, I mean Tricia, found one under her step the day before she disappeared."

"Did she?" Zach tears his eyes away from my pocket to look at me in surprise.

"She never mentioned that to you?"

"No, never. We were partying pretty hard that night, though. She was wasted."

I'm glad for the arrival of my food so I don't have to speak for a few minutes. No matter how many times I hear it, I can't wrap my head around the idea of Pat partying. She's had this road map for her life for as long as I can remember — work hard, go to an Ivy League school on a full ride, study marine ecology, save the world. And she was not a girl for detours. Even Mark was part of The Plan. Presentable, but not too good-looking. Grateful for the tiny corner of her life she let him inhabit. She could take him to events that required a boyfriend and park him when she didn't need him. I always thought he got a raw deal, but that's the thing about Pat, she's like a meteor rocketing through your life. You grab on to what you can, even if all you're left with is cosmic dust.

"Did Pat often get wasted?" I ask. Is it possible Tracy was right? Maybe Pat was getting threatened by someone who left the doll under her step to scare her. "Did she seem upset that night?"

Zach looks out at the street. It's still early; most of the shops haven't opened, but there are already lots of people around — old ladies sweeping, a man pushing an empty cart toward the pier, some dreadlocked teenagers looking like they haven't been to bed yet. Zach leans one arm on the porch railing as he considers my question.

"Maybe," he says finally.

"So tell me," I demand.

"It was like weeks ago, man, and I was stoned. . . ."

"Just tell me what you remember, buddy." I force my voice to remain calm. "Do it for Tricia."

"Well, it's just that the night she disappeared, she was drinking, but she wasn't drinking like her, you know?"

"She wasn't drinking like her?"

"Yeah."

"You're losing me, Zach. If she wasn't drinking like her, who was she drinking like?"

"Me," he says solemnly.

I think about this for a moment. "You mean, she was drinking a lot? So she didn't normally drink a lot? Just that night?"

"Exactamundo." He crosses his arms on the table and puts his head down. The effort of remembering has taken it out of him.

"You okay, buddy?"

He lifts his head and passes a hand over his eyes. Tears are seeping out. I exhale slowly before getting up to go round the table and pat his back. I should be charging for the amount of time I spend cleaning up the fallout of my sister's recklessness. This was just supposed to be a simple summer gig. She'd get a bit of work experience, spend some time with the fish she loves so much and, most important, get a break from our mother. She wasn't supposed to take up drinking or fall for some local guy. And she sure as hell had no business swimming at night, all by herself, after a night of drinking.

ME: *What were you doing, Pat? How could you let things get so out of control?*

PAT: *Suck it up, little brother. You spent seventeen years letting me deal with Mom and every other problem that came our way. Don't you think I deserved a bit of fun?*

ME: *What was fun about getting drunk and jumping in the ocean at night?*

PAT: *Well, you're the authority on getting drunk. You tell me.*

ME:

"Come on, Zach." I stand up. "Let's pay the bill and get out of here."

Zach pulls himself together, and we go inside to look for our waiter. We find him on the back porch, which is built right up against a steep wall of rock that's part of the town hill. Zach insists on running back to our table to fetch food remnants for the iguanas that he claims live in the rocks. I'm skeptical, but sure enough, when he returns with a bit of bacon and tosses it across the railing, massive reptiles emerge from every nook and cranny.

"I love this place." Zach grins, and I'm so grateful to see him happy again that I grin right back. "We need Lemon Larry," he says as we leave the restaurant.

"Lemon Larry?"

"Yeah. He's this guy who's lived here for like thirty years, and he's always talking about this witch-doctor lady he visits way out in the bush somewhere. I don't know if she's practicing voodoo, but it's definitely something like that. If Pat got a doll and disappeared and now you have a doll, we've got to get help quick before you disappear, too."

I doubt I'm in any real danger, but it's very likely that the same person who tried to scare my sister is now trying to scare me, and that's a lead I can't ignore. "Do you know where this Larry guy lives?"

"Yeah, but he won't be there. He has breakfast at the Crackerjack."

So in this town not only do you see everyone you know, but you see them so often you learn their routines. I understand now why Dr. Jake was convinced something was wrong when Pat didn't show up for her shift. Ten minutes of walking through the town, twenty if he stopped to chat with people, and he'd know she was well and truly missing.

We walk for a full three minutes before hitting the restaurant where Lemon Larry eats with such frequency that the pattern has penetrated even Zach's brain. I follow Zach up the steps and remind myself to ask him why every restaurant, hotel and most homes are built on stilts several feet above the ground. Zach weaves through the tables and slides onto a bench opposite a man with wrinkled brown skin the consistency of bark (obviously not a fan of sunscreen), but with startling blue eyes and a shock of blond hair. I'm guessing some Scandinavian blood, but when he starts talking, it's impossible to be sure.

"Zachary, my mate, where you been hiding yourself? I haven't seen you for days." They high-five.

"Had to go to Ceiba, on the mainland," says Zach.

"Ah, well done, lad! After some Spanish lovin', were ya? The mainland girls are the best. Most of them don't speak a word of English. So much the better, I say."

"Not exactly."

"Get as much as you can while you're young, lad. No lady can resist a hard body. And who's this handsome fellow? How you doing, boy?" He holds out his hand.

"This is Luke and he needs to see your friend, Lemon. The lady bush doctor."

"Like that, is it? Well don't worry, lad. So what's the problem? Can't get it up? Don't worry, she'll fix you right quick." He leans forward and whispers confidentially, "Had to take the cure myself a few times."

"He doesn't have that problem!" Zach exclaims.

"Oh, I see, the other then, is it? You need a love potion?" Lemon gives me a sympathetic look. "Strapping boy like you, I should have known. Your girl caught you with someone else, did she?"

"He got a doll."

"A doll?" Lemon shakes his head. "That's not going to work. She's not a kid. It's going to take a lot more than a doll to get back in her pants."

"Someone put a hex on him."

"Well, that's a shame. Some girls are just spiteful. Are you sure she's worth the trouble?"

"Actually," I say, "the thing is —"

"Can your bush doctor friend get the spell off him?" Zach interrupts.

"Likely, but don't tell her what you did to deserve the hex, Luke, my boy. Had the very same problem last year. Needed a love potion for the Missus. Old Martha sold me the potion, then right down the river. Told the Missus everything."

"Where can we find Martha?" I ask.

"I'll draw you a map. She lives deep in the bush, so you want to set out early. It wouldn't do to get caught out there after dark. There are crocs in the inner lagoons. Damn tree-huggers have brought 'em back from the brink of extinction. All well and good till you find yourself providing 'em dinner."

Lemon draws a complicated map on his paper napkin. In place of street names, he puts down landmarks, like Fentiman's Folly and Blackish Point. He walks Zach through it. I try to follow, but it's clear I'm going to need Zach's help to find the place.

"Stay on dry land" is Lemon's final instruction. "If your feet are wet, you're too far west. She's a fair piece off the road, but she's on the edge of the swamp, not in it."

Fifteen minutes later, we're walking out of there. Zach has the napkin in his pocket.

"Can't go till this afternoon," says Zach. "If I don't help with the dive this morning, I'm fired."

"No problem. Meet you later, then?"

It'll give me time to grill Jamie on his relationship with Pat. I might even bring up the voodoo doll, though if he did put it under my step, he's not likely to admit it. We walk together toward Bluewater, since the Shark Center's just beyond.

The heat's already making the air shimmer, and wet patches form under my arms. I'm out of clean shirts. Maybe I should do a wash before I head up the hill to look for Jamie. I could use another shower as well. For the first time, I look with longing at the snatches of aquamarine ocean peeking out from between buildings.

"I need to bring in some new divers," says Zach.

Okay, not that much longing.

"Good luck with that."

"There's no one on the island who isn't already certified or signed up for courses."

I glance at him and wish I hadn't. He gives me a pleading look. "Sorry," I say and speed up a little. We're almost at Bluewater.

"You wouldn't have to do the whole course."

"I'm not going in the ocean, Zach. I'm sorry."

"We could stay in the shallow water, near the shore."

"Sharks can attack in less than two feet of water."

"The sharks like the reef. We'll stay in the sandy area."

"Cone shells bury themselves in the sand and shoot out their teeth like spearguns," I say.

"You'd be wearing flippers."

"Lionfish are moving south from Florida."

"The water's so clear, you'd see them a mile away."

"What about the voodoo doll?"

He stops walking. "Oh, man." Zach slaps his forehead and looks at me in horror. "I totally forgot you were hexed. How could I forget that? I'm so sorry."

"It's okay," I say, biting my lip to stop from smiling.

"It's not okay. We're like brothers now. I should have your back and I almost killed you."

"You didn't almost kill me."

"I did, brother, I totally did. You would have got bitten by a shark for sure and had one of the cone things stab you and a lionfish sting you, and it would've been all my fault."

"Probably not all those things would have happened." Though knowing my luck, at least one of them would have.

"You need to go back to your room and stay there. Okay? I'll come get you after my dive."

"Sure," I agree. I'll stay in my room, right after I shower, wash some clothes and talk to Jamie.

"And don't open the door for anyone till I come back."

"Okay."

"We need a code word."

"A code word?"

"Yeah. Like how will you know it's me at the door and not a voodoo zombie pretending to be me? We definitely need a code word. Something a voodoo zombie wouldn't think of. What should I say?" He gives me an earnest look.

"Cosmic?" I suggest.

"Yeah." Zach grins and puts up his hand for a high five. "Cosmic. That's genius. Who would ever think of it?"

"Almost no one," I deadpan.

"Okay, I won't fail you a second time, my brother. Just wait for the code word."

CHAPTER 6

I run into Reesie when I step out of the shower room wrapped in my towel. I'm holding all three of my shirts and my only shorts, freshly laundered with bath soap. Reesie's got her pail and cleaning brush and gives me an irritated look before she tries to push past me.

"We've got to stop meeting like this." I smile, deliberately stepping into her path.

"Don't bother trying your flirting on me." She scowls.

"I was hoping to talk to your brother this morning." I keep my tone friendly, but this girl's as cuddly as a sea urchin.

"He's gone to the cays. Won't be back till tomorrow."

"The cays?"

"Yeah, you know, the little islands just west of here. The *cays*," she enunciates. When I don't respond, she shakes her head in disgust and brushes past me into the shower room.

I stand there listening to her fill her pail. I was really counting on talking to Jamie this morning. Zach's revelation that Pat was drinking a lot on her last night makes me think she must have been upset about something. Of course, she could have been celebrating. Either way, the most likely person to know her state of mind is her alleged fiancé.

Something's biting me. I suddenly notice tiny red spots covering my chest and arms. What the hell?

Reesie emerges from the shower room and pauses when she notices me examining myself. "They really got you," she observes.

"What are *they*?"

"You really don't know anything, do you?"

I shrug.

"Sand flies. The bites'll start itching fierce in about twenty-four hours. You want to get yourself some medicine before then. Some people find salt water helps. You planning on swimming?"

"Not likely," I say.

She cocks a brow. "Tea tree oil might help. You can pick it up most anywhere, but if you want to get away from 'em right now, there's a strong wind at the end of the dock."

I look down the path to the dock and notice for the first time that the Shark Center boat is out. It must have left while I was in the shower. The sun looks hot on the dock, but it might dry my clothes faster. I can't go anywhere till I have something to wear.

"Thanks," I say. "Will you tell your brother I need to speak to him?"

"He knows that." She smirks. "You told him yourself last night when you were . . . busy."

I blink. "Right, well, see ya." I stomp past her down to the dock and walk straight to the end.

The water beneath me looks about ten feet deep but could be deeper. The ocean's so clear, it's like looking into your bathtub, if you had creepy coral heads and bizarre fish in your tub. Near the shore it's pale blue; then, about thirty feet out, it gets darker all of a sudden. The coral's still visible, but it's shadowy, like monsters lurking under the bed. If a shark attacked in this water, you'd see it coming long before it bit you. You'd still be dead, but it'd be quite the sight.

The wind is strong and I can't feel the pricks of sand flies anymore, so I lay out my clothes and settle down to enjoy a few moments of relief. There are at least fifty docks, some only a few feet apart, jutting out from one end of the town to the other in a curve around a natural harbor. There's constant coming and going, mostly fishing and dive boats leaving and narrow rickety dories arriving, a few loaded with people but most with a single boatman. Like the buildings in town, most of these boats have peeling paint and chunks out of them. They don't look very seaworthy, but the grizzled captains handle them with relaxed confidence.

I hang my legs over the edge of the dock and watch a steady parade of fish swim underneath. The colors and shapes are amazing. My sister had some unusual fish in her aquariums but nothing like this. There's a couple I've only seen in books — big boxy things, with elaborate spots and patches. I pull my feet up fast as a huge dark shape approaches from the deep. It's about five feet wide and quite a bit longer, with winglike fins that undulate slowly. My heart speeds up as it glides beneath me, turns under the dock and swims out again. It's the first time I've seen an eagle ray in the flesh.

PAT: *The spots look like constellations in the night sky.*
ME: *You know those things leap into boats and kill people.*

PAT: *Freak events. How often does that happen?*

ME: *Do you want the national stats or worldwide?*

PAT: *You used to love sea life as much as I did. We watched* National Geographic *specials together. You read almost every book I did.*

ME: *That's the difference between you and me, Pat. Just because I read about a dangerous activity doesn't mean I want to try it. You act like nothing's ever going to hurt you. I would have thought living with a depressed alcoholic mother would have given you a more realistic perspective.*

PAT: *Is that what it gave you, Luke? Or are you just a coward drowning your fears in booze and drugs?*

ME:

"What're you doing out here all by yourself?"

I look up in surprise to see Reesie looming over me.

"I'm drying my clothes." I prepare to be told off again, even though it was her idea I come out here. If I'm breaking some kind of moral code sitting here in nothing but a towel, she should have thought of that earlier. Not to mention the fact that Tracy didn't have a bikini line. What does that tell you about the local dress code? I may not bring that example up, though.

She doesn't say anything, just plops down beside me and joins my fish-watching. She's probably trying to get my guard down before launching another attack.

"That's not what I meant." She takes off her sandals, swinging her bare feet over the water. "What are you doing here in Utila?"

"We've had this conversation. I'm looking for my sister, remember?"

"No." She turns to me and doesn't continue until I look at her, which I take my time doing. "Your parents already lost one child. Why'd they let you come here, alone?"

I look away fast.

The ray has circled back and wings under us again. It's strange that it keeps returning to the dock.

"Their pups are born with everything they'll ever need to survive," I say. "They have a barb on the end of their tail to protect them, they know how to find food and their mouth plates are fully formed. They don't need their parents for anything."

"All you tourist kids think about is fish."

"But no one knows why they jump. Sometimes the females jump when they're giving birth and the pups drop out of them in midair. Some people think they jump to evade predators."

"They probably jump because they're bored," says Reesie.

"I didn't think they'd let me come," I confess. "I didn't ask them until after I'd bought the ticket, but even so, right up until I walked in the room and told Mom to put down her drink, I thought one of them would stop me."

"They didn't try?" She's doing a poor job of keeping her voice neutral.

"My dad asked if I had enough cash. Mom didn't say anything. I think she was happy to see me go. It's not like I was doing anything important back home, and they're as anxious for me to find Pat as I am." I pause to focus on breathing as tightness spreads across my chest. I know I shouldn't feel hurt

that my parents let me go off alone to the same place Pat disappeared. They'd already been down here ahead of me, so
they probably felt comfortable it wasn't dangerous; but if
they believed that, what do they think happened to Pat?

"Anyway, Mom's got her own problems," I say, as much
to myself as to Reesie. "She can't be worrying about me all
the time." I'm hoping Reesie will leave it at that and not push
me to explain that Mom never seemed to worry about me,
not when I cut school or got suspended for smoking dope —
not even when I got busted for selling fake IDs and she and
Dad had to come down to the police station to bail me out.
She told me not to do it again, but she never got angry and
she never once punished me. That was weird, because Pat
could make the smallest mistake — oversleep and miss swim
practice or get a B on a test — and Mom would be all over
her. Maybe she figured with me there was no point. I've
never been particularly good in school. I don't have my sister's brains or ambition.

I feel every contour of the wood as my hands grip the
dock. Reesie covers my hand with hers, and we sit like that
for a while. I can feel her waiting, and a part of me would
like to spill my whole life story. I imagine it would be a relief
to talk it out with someone, and as bad tempered as Reesie
is, there's something solid about her. I feel I can trust her. But
I'm scared if I start talking, I might not know where to stop.

I'm quiet for a long while. This girl is patient; I'll say that
for her.

"Pat has a scholarship to study marine biology in the
fall," I continue finally. "It's everything she's always wanted,
everything she's worked for, but she came here instead."

"But just for the summer, right?" asks Reesie.

"Sure," I say unconvincingly. "But the thing is, she didn't need to come here at all. If she'd stuck to her own plan, she'd be safe at home right now."

"So she took a detour. I expect most of the tourist kids here are doing that. It's not so surprising, is it?"

"But that's not like her. From as far back as I can remember, she had this plan for her life. She never deviated, never hesitated, until the last couple of months. Things changed." I hesitate, trying to figure out how to explain, without telling her everything. I'm not sure what I want from her; absolution, maybe, though I know it's not hers to give. "Pat never really had much chance to be a kid. The first time it dawned on me our mom might not be up to the job of parenting us was when she forgot to pick me up from kindergarten on my first day of school. Pat was only six, but she showed up at the classroom door and made the teacher let me go home with her. I threw a tantrum, wanting to wait for my mom, but Pat insisted Mom wasn't coming. Turns out she was right. Mom had fallen asleep watching her daytime soaps. It was years of that kind of thing before I realized she had a drinking problem, but I think Pat always knew."

"My daddy died a few months ago," says Reesie quietly. "He was working on a ship off the coast of West Africa and took a fever."

I turn to her but she's staring down at the water, so I flip my hand over and curl my fingers through hers.

"How old are you?" I ask.

"Sixteen." She says it like a challenge, like it might be too old for something or too young.

"Don't you go to school?"

She looks at me then, her eyes blazing.

"You really are dumb, aren't you?" She snatches her hand away. "Didn't I just tell you my daddy died? You think my family's got money to send me to school now?" She scrambles to her feet.

I leap to mine, ready with an apology. My towel does not leap with me.

"Ah," I say.

"You dropped something," she says.

"Right." I snatch up my towel and hastily wrap it around my waist.

The first attempt only somewhat covers my butt, and one end hangs ineffectively down my leg. My equipment is still feeling the cooling breeze off the Caribbean. I turn my back on her to make some strategic adjustments.

"Everything all right over there?" she asks sweetly. I can tell she's enjoying this.

Would it be ungallant to shove her off the dock? She's an islander; I'm sure she can swim.

"Fine," I snap.

When I turn around, she's sitting down again, swinging her bare feet and grinning.

I hesitate. I don't much feel like sitting with her anymore, but I don't have anything else to do. I thump down and resume my fish watch.

"So why did your sister come out here if that wasn't in her plan?" she asks.

"She and my mom fought all the time. Mom was always pushing her. Nothing Pat did was ever good enough." I'm not sure how to explain why Mom was so hard on Pat when I never really understood it myself. "Don't get me wrong. She's proud of Pat. She used to brag about her all the time when Pat wasn't around. She had a box in her room where she saved every one of Pat's report cards and every award. I found it once when I was looking through her closet." I don't mention I was rifling through Mom's pockets for cash to buy drugs. "I don't think Pat ever knew about the box, and I never told her either. I wish I'd told her, but I don't know if it would have made any difference. As angry as Mom was at Pat, Pat gave it back a hundred times over. I think it might have enraged Pat more to think Mom was hoarding proof of her achievements — like Mom was trying to share credit for her success."

"It must have been hard to be in the middle of that," Reesie says sympathetically, taking my hand again.

I give her a crooked smile. "I don't know if I'd say I was in the middle, exactly; more like on the sidelines, worrying about how it was all going to play out." I don't tell her that sometimes I envied Pat her battles with Mom. How twisted is that? But at least Mom noticed her.

"So you supported Pat coming here to get away from your mom?"

"Something like that," I say, feeling my face heat up. I look away.

"I'm really sorry I said mean things about her," Reesie says. "I only saw her drunk once or twice and, even then, she wasn't really drunk. And she was always nice to me, not like some. She gave me a book once. Sounds stupid, but that really meant something to me. I came in to clean her room and she was reading it. I asked her if it was good and she offered to give it to me when she was done. Didn't occur to her I might not be much of a reader. Fact is, I used to love reading when I was in school, but I'd kind of lost sight of that in the last little while. I read that book from cover to cover. I kept meaning to tell her how much I liked it. I had this plan that maybe we'd discuss it a little; maybe I'd even ask if I could borrow another. It was probably a dumb idea anyway."

"Why? I'm sure she would have liked that."

"I don't know. The kids who come here don't necessarily think about us like that."

I give her a quizzical look but she grimaces. I think maybe she's wishing she hadn't started.

"Come on. I told you stuff." I grin playfully.

She grins back but immediately ducks her head. "I think the kids who come here don't see us as real people," she says. "Maybe it's because they think they're more educated or because they've traveled. Maybe it's because we're always picking up after them in one way or another. I can't explain it, but there's this divide. They come here with their drugs and their drinking and are rowdy till all hours. And we go to church, look after our families and try to make a living. It's like, for them, Utila is a break from real life but, for us, this island is our life."

I look down at her slim brown fingers laced through my own and try to feel the truth of what she's saying. She's the first person in a long while I've actually wanted to connect to in a way that wasn't mostly about sex or getting high. And just because she cleans cabins for a living doesn't mean that's who she is. I want to tell her this. I don't know how to put it into words, though, without sounding preachy or lame.

"I best be getting back to work," she says abruptly, pulling her hand out of mine.

"You know why I think eagle rays jump?" I say quickly, wanting to hold her back and explain something that's been brewing in me since Pat left. "I think sometimes they just want to see what other possibilities are out there. Sometimes the ocean is just too small."

Reesie takes my hand again and looks me right in the eye. "Even if your sister was set on getting away from your family, it doesn't mean she wanted to leave you."

"Maybe," I say, wondering how long her sympathy would last if I told her the whole story of how my sister ended up here. I want to tell her. I think it might feel good to finally get it off my chest, but just as the words are forming, we're interrupted by the sound of the Shark Center boat pulling up to the dock.

"Catch the line," Pete shouts, throwing me a rope from the front of the boat.

"I thought you were gone for the day." I stand up carefully, so as not to dislodge my towel, and catch the rope, hesitating because I'm not an expert on nautical knots.

"Tie it up," Pete orders, so I do. If the boat drifts away, he has only himself to blame.

He jumps off and ties up the back.

"What are you doing out here?" he demands. "Bonding with Reesie?" I notice for the first time that she's already off the dock and heading down the footpath, pail in hand.

"Is that a problem?" I ask.

He smirks like it's a big joke. "It's none of my business."

"You got that right."

Fishboy's an asshole, but I can't get on the wrong side of him until I've found out what he knows about Pat.

"You need any help?" I ask.

"You a diver?"

"Not exactly."

"Would you mind hauling some tanks to the boat? That would be great."

"Sure thing. I'll be right back."

I take my clothes to my room, throw on my shorts and a T-shirt and head out to the shed where they keep the dive gear. Pete's hauling out tanks. He gives me the job of loading weights into the dive belts. Despite the number of years Pat's been diving, I've never looked closely at the equipment before. Each nylon belt has a row of pockets to snugly encase half a dozen solid lead weights.

"You mean people actually leap into the water with these on?" I ask, as I heave a handful of weighted belts over my shoulder to haul down to the dock.

"Have to. The oxygen and the dive suit make you float in the water, but you pile on enough weights and anyone will sink like a stone."

I shake my head. I will never understand the appeal of this sport. We don't say much else for the next twenty minutes as we load the boat and Pete drones on about their special air-powered motor that doesn't disturb the sharks. Apparently, he hasn't considered that with 332 million cubic miles of ocean, the sharks can just swim away if they're disturbed.

I fit the last of the tanks into one of the wooden slots that line both sides of the boat and sit down on the hard bench that runs in front of it. The boat is cramped but okay, I guess, for people who are going to spend most of their day in the water. Pete has disappeared into a tiny cabin at the front with an enormous supply of junk food. He appears to be one of those guys who likes to prepare for every emergency, like an overpowering Cheetos craving when they're out on the high seas.

Finally, he climbs out and stands next to me. "Thanks for your help. You should come out with us today. Jake wouldn't charge you."

"Tempting, but I have other plans."

"What? You got a date with Reesie?" He smirks. Again.

Keep it up, Fishboy, and you'll be seeing more marine life than you bargained for.

"How well did you know my sister?" I say in an even voice. He flops down next to me and props his feet up on the center bench.

"We didn't really hang out, if that's what you're asking. We got along well at work."

"Did you see her the night she disappeared?"

He hesitates and scratches an insect bite on his arm.

"I saw her at the Spiny Starfish. We were all pretty hammered. I might have chatted with her a bit, but I didn't see her leave." He runs his hand through his hair, tousling it to perfect his surfer look. "I really am sorry for what happened to her."

"What did happen to her?" I shoot back, hoping to catch him off guard. I've got no reason to suspect he's involved, but the guy rubs me the wrong way.

He jumps to his feet, arches his back and rolls his shoulders in a languorous stretch that somehow looks like he's doing it for my benefit. "I'd love to continue this conversation, but I've really got to get this show on the road." His smile doesn't reach his eyes. "We're supposed to be heading out by ten. I've already got divers waiting in the office."

I get up too. The space between the benches is narrow and we're squared off, almost touching, chest to chest.

"Do you know what happened to my sister?" I demand, my face inches from his own.

He leans past me and tests the air pressure on one of the tanks. We both listen to the air whoosh out. He straightens.

"No, I don't," he says, and for the first time since we started talking, he actually looks me in the eye. "I honestly wish I did."

He hops up on the bench and, with a second jump, he's off the boat and striding down the dock with the easy rhythm of an athlete, a jock, the kind of guy who's always hitting on my sister. What these guys never understand is, she doesn't care about the rippling muscles, and she downright hates the smug swagger that oozes out of them like stink. If Pete had made any kind of play for my sister, she would have turned him down flat.

I flex my arms, stretching out the muscles that coil every time I'm near this guy. There's something about him that's off.

But is he lying?

CHAPTER 7

ike every other building I've seen in Utila, the Spiny
Starfish is constructed of wooden clapboard and, like
most, the salt air hasn't been good to it. I walk up the
steps past a padlocked room, presumably the kitchen, onto a
veranda that extends way out over the sea. Sharing a wall
with the kitchen is a fully stocked open-air bar, with a brick
pizza oven at one end; beyond that are wooden picnic tables
that look sturdy but uncomfortable. There's a guy asleep on
one of them. Other than him, the place is empty.

I'm debating whether I should wake him when he rolls
over and opens one eye.

"Yo," he calls over to me. "You wanna bring me a coffee?"

I look around, like maybe there was a Starbucks I didn't
notice on the way in.

"The bar." He waves an arm.

When I walk behind the bar, sure enough, there's a cof-
feemaker with a coffee can sitting beside it. As luck would
have it, coffee is something I know how to make: the silver
lining of having a mother who's a drunk. I rifle through the
fridge for milk. There isn't any, nor is there sugar, though

I find an impressive array of cream liqueurs. I pull out a coconut cream concoction and examine the label. After a few minutes, the coffee stops gurgling so I pour two cups and consider the liqueur again. There's something to be said for the hair of the dog. But not much. I decide my new friend has had enough alcohol. I tip some into my cup, though.

He doesn't stir as I walk over, which doesn't surprise me since he's obviously slept right through the shrieks of kids who are swimming off the next dock. I put down both cups, settle at a nearby table and clear my throat.

He turns over. Bulging muscles strain against the fabric of his Hawaiian shirt. If he's the watchman, he's in the wrong line of work.

"I got some java juice here, buddy," I say.

He opens his eyes, rubs them and rolls to a sitting position, resting his feet on the bench. I'm amazed at how easily he wakes up. I usually have to resort to threats with Mom. I hand him a cup and watch him take a slow sip as he passes a hand over his close-cropped 'fro.

"Put something extra in yours, did ya?" He eyes me speculatively over the top of his cup.

I shrug.

"I always wonder about a man who drinks before noon," he says.

"I always wonder about a man who passes out on a picnic table."

"You got balls, I'll give you that. So what you doing in my establishment at this time of day?"

I'm surprised to hear he's the owner, but I give him a sphinxlike stare.

He chuckles. "What? You think I was the hired help?"

Perhaps not totally sphinxlike.

"I just thought, you know, being passed out drunk and all . . ."

I swear I'm sounding more like my sister every day.

A roar rips out of him.

I jump. It takes a moment to register that he's laughing. I smile. Nervously.

"I was serving till 3:00 a.m., didn't get the place cleared till well past four." He pauses and looks me up and down. "I could use a strong guy like you. You looking for work?"

"Just information."

He cocks his head.

"This was the last place my sister was seen, the night she disappeared."

"You Tricia's brother?" His gravelly voice is a mixture of shock and concern.

"Yeah," I say and get straight to the point. "Do you remember anything about her that night?"

"Not much," he says slowly and turns away to watch the kids cannonballing into the water, competing to make the biggest splash.

I follow his gaze and all at once I'm reminded of the last visit to my grandparents' cottage before Pat decided we were severing all contact. She was ten.

ME: *Do you remember that visit? Mom was arguing with Nana and Grandpa. It was dusk, and we were all out on the dock. You dove into the lake and swam way out past the buoys. They didn't even notice.*

PAT: *I just needed some peace and quiet. They'd been fighting all weekend.*

ME: *I screamed at you to come back — you were out too deep. It got dark and I couldn't see you anymore. The adults took the fight indoors, but I stayed on the dock waiting. I started thinking maybe you couldn't come back. Maybe something had attacked you.*

PAT: *Attacked me? In Lake Michigan?*

ME: *Don't you remember telling me about the bull sharks?*

PAT: *Not really. What did I say?*

ME: *You told me bull sharks are the only sharks that can adapt to freshwater. And there'd been attacks in Lake Michigan, our lake.*

PAT: *I do remember reading that, but it hasn't been absolutely verified. Anyway, you couldn't really have thought a bull shark got me. There's been like two unconfirmed reports in recorded history. I was just teasing you.*

ME: *I kept searching the darkness for a fin. A dozen times I was sure I saw one. I wondered if I'd even hear you scream. It might have pulled you under too fast or taken off your leg. You could have been in shock and bleeding out. I didn't know whether to go for help or go in after you, but what if it got me, too? I shouted for you until my throat was raw.*

PAT: *I knew you'd been crying when I got back to the dock. I tried to apologize, but you wouldn't even speak to me.*

ME: *They're one of the most dangerous sharks after great whites. They attack unprovoked and they hunt at night.*

PAT: *You always did have a great imagination.*

ME: *I was nine, Pat, and you were the one person in my life I could always count on.*

PAT: *But I was never in danger, Luke. Sure, bull sharks sometimes end up in odd places, but really, what were the chances?*

ME: *Chance has never been on our side, Pat.*

PAT: *Is that when it started?*

ME: *My drinking? What do you think? You took the vodka away from me later that night.*

PAT: *Not the drinking, your phobia. You never wanted to go in the water after that. You always made some excuse.*

ME:

"Anything you can tell me about her would help," I say.

"She was in here a lot," he says, still watching the kids. "Couldn't get enough of my barbecued chicken, you know?"

"No," I say, feeling suddenly tired. "Patricia's been a vegan since she was old enough to say 'Hold the mayo.' So, no, I really don't know."

He looks at me in surprise. "Vegans eat meat-lovers' pizza?"

I sigh.

"Did you know she had a boyfriend?" he asks, taking a gulp of his coffee.

"I know about Jamie," I say.

He smiles in relief. "Jamie's a friend. I promised not to spread it around that they were going together. I think he was worried his family might not approve, but you can't get much warmer people than Utilans. They've accepted the likes of me, all the way from Africa, and that's saying something." He gives his bellowing laugh again but then turns serious. "I guess you know Tricia and Jamie fought that night, then?" I try not to look surprised.

"Jamie didn't go into all the details," I say carefully.

"I don't imagine there's much more I can tell you. We were busy that night. They came in happy, but he left early and she stayed on. She was really knocking them back hard. That's how I figured they'd been fighting. Your sister likes a drink, but she knows her limits."

The way I see it, she'd been pushing her limits with a lot more than alcohol.

"Who was she with after Jamie left?"

He looks at me steadily. "Sorry, I couldn't tell you. I don't know all the dive kids. One of the girls who works for me might know, though. Jamie came by later that night asking the same questions you are."

"I appreciate your help." I fight to keep the disappointment out of my voice.

"Come back some evening and talk to the girls. They might have seen something."

I nod.

Finishing the last of my spiked coffee, I stand up, get a rush of blood to my head, grab the table for support and wait for the dizziness to subside. With the heat and my lack of sleep, the alcohol might not have been the best idea. I should probably go back to my room and crash for a bit, but I head to Bluewater. Lemon said we should get an early start to the bush-doctor lady and it's already nearly midday. Maybe Zach's back from his dive and we can get going.

Out on the road, I feel my pocket to make sure the voodoo doll is still where I put it after I washed my shorts. I shake my head at the notion that it might be anywhere else. Zach's conviction that it has supernatural powers must have me more rattled than I thought.

The road's busy now, with bicycles, motorcycles and golf carts competing with pedestrians for the limited space. I duck into a store to buy water and get distracted by the surprising array of options on the shelves. It's stifling, with only a couple of ceiling fans pushing around the humid air, and it's small, even by convenience-store standards, but there's a bit of everything and a lot of familiar brand names. I pick up an ice-cream pop as well as the water. The girl at the cash gives me the price in Spanish, which, of course, I don't understand, but I read it off her register and count out the change in lempiras.

Ten minutes later, I'm sitting on the dock at Bluewater, having learned that their dive boat's still out but due back soon. The fish life here isn't nearly as varied as under the shark dock. There's a school of round, blue, disc-shaped fish and a couple of long pipefish but no rays or boxy things. I swing my legs off the dock in relative confidence they won't be ripped from my body and wave at passing boatmen because every single one of them waves at me. It gets old after the third or fourth time, so I decide to lie down and give my eyes a rest.

The dock is hard, and I have to shift around a bit to avoid getting jabbed by protruding nails. I don't plan on sleeping, but the next thing I know, Zach is shaking me awake in the middle of a dream where I'm making out with the hot Swedish chick. I'm glad he woke me because the Swedish chick had just morphed into Reesie, who did not look pleased to discover my hand up her shirt. I take a minute to catch my breath, my heart still racing, and notice the sun's moved considerably in the sky. It's got to be well past noon.

"Dude, I told you not to leave your room," says Zach, looking worried.

"Yeah." I try to shake off the memory of me and Reesie up close and personal. "Sorry. I got bored."

"Well, you're not hurt or anything," Zach admits, though he doesn't sound convinced. "Help me haul in this gear and we can get going."

He climbs back in the boat and picks up a tank, holding it aloft. "Grab it," he shouts.

I jump up to help him but stand aside for a couple of divers scrambling off. They're going on about rays and turtles. I don't tell them they could have seen just as much sitting on the shark dock without risking their lives. Zach wasn't joking about business being slow. The captain and three dive masters, including Zach, outnumber the paying divers. I'm not surprised his job's on the line, and I feel a stab of guilt that I refused to sign up with him. For the next ten minutes, I overcompensate by working twice as fast as any of them, hauling gear.

"You're the best, Luke," says Zach, standing back in admiration as I walk past him lugging tanks, two at a time.

"Go have your shower," I say. "I'll get the rest of this."

"Cosmic," says Zach, his eyes shining. I don't think he has a lot of experience with people doing nice things for him. I'm mostly just trying to ease my own conscience, but I'm really glad it makes him happy.

"Glad to help," I say.

I carry the last of the tanks into the dive shack, where a petite girl in a tiny string bikini is loading fins and masks into a large concrete sink. No question, there are some advantages to island living.

"I'm Luke." I give her a friendly smile as I set down the tanks next to the dozen or so already there. "You might have known my sister, Patricia."

"Oh, wow, sure." She looks at me with sympathy. "Zach told me you were here searching for her. I'm so sorry."

I feel a rush of hope. At least she knows Pat. It's a start, though given the size of the island and the fact that they're in related lines of work, it would probably be more surprising if she didn't.

"You didn't happen to be at the Spiny Starfish the night she disappeared, did you?"

"Sure, we've all talked about how weird it was. One minute she was there and the next she wasn't. It was like she just vanished. . . ."

She turns away, busying herself with rinsing equipment. I'm disappointed, but she could still know something important, even if she doesn't think she does.

"Did you see who she was with?"

She turns back and furrows her brow. "A lot of people. She was talking to a guy from the Shark Center for quite a while. I don't remember his name."

"Pete?" I ask, trying not to sound too eager.

"Yeah," she says slowly. "I think so. He seemed way into her, but it was totally one-sided. You know what I mean? He was practically climbing onto her lap, and she looked like she wanted to be anywhere but there. I think she had a boyfriend, didn't she?"

"Yeah, so I've been told."

"Well, for what it's worth, that Shark Center guy didn't look like he was giving up easily."

"Did she seem scared of him?" I'm not sure what answer I want to hear, but she shakes her head.

"No, not all, she just looked irritated and a bit bored. I guess that's why she took off."

"But you didn't see her leave?"

"No, like I said, the guy was pawing her and she kept pushing him off. The next time I looked over, she was gone."

She returns her attention to the sink and starts transferring the rinsed equipment onto a nearby shelf. I think about how much I'd like to run straight back to the Shark Center and beat the shit out of Pete. Instead I pitch in and help, to give her some time in case she remembers something else. It's frustrating how many people saw Pat on her last night, some even realizing she was upset, but no one caring enough to notice when she walked out of their lives. I know they couldn't have anticipated she was going to disappear; I just wish someone had asked her why she was drinking so much or had told Pete to leave her alone.

I don't believe Pete's unwanted attention would have made Pat do something crazy. She was used to getting hit on. Even a fight with Jamie wouldn't have pushed her over the edge. Pat's seen way more drama in our home life than anyone here could throw at her, and I know she doesn't fall apart easily, but I'm beginning to get an idea of her last night and I don't like it one bit. My sister needed help and no one on this island gave it to her.

We continue to work in silence. She rinses equipment while I sort it by function — fins in one bin, masks in another, dive weights stacked on a shelf above them next to belts and respirators, suits and dive vests hung to dry. Finally, Zach pops his head in the door. "Let's go, brother. It's time to rock and roll."

I give the girl a polite nod, even though, unfair as it is, I'm feeling angry at her for not rescuing Pat. She thanks me for my help and tells me again how she sorry is. It seems heartfelt, and I feel guilty for blaming her. It's not like I'm in any doubt who's really to blame.

CHAPTER 8

I notice Zach has a very full pack for a quick hike into the bush.

"What you got in there?" I ask as we stride down the main road.

"Nectar of the gods," says Zach mysteriously.

"Beer?"

"No, man." He looks offended for a nanosecond before a thought occurs to him and he smiles sheepishly. "Well, yeah, that, too. But I brought something even more important." He pauses, thinks for a minute. "Equally important," he amends and swings his pack off his shoulder so he can reach one hand in to yank out a bottle.

"Bug juice," he crows, punching the air with it. "You should put some on right away. You may already have bites."

I look down at my arms, covered in red marks that are starting to swell.

"A few," I say, taking the bottle from him. I spray as we walk, wincing as the bug poison soaks into some of the bites I've scratched raw.

We have to cut across the island, which means taking the road straight up the hill from the pier. We pass the turnoff for Reesie's house, and in minutes we're walking past farms and then deserted bush. Next to the road, the trees are scrubby, but as the paved road curves round toward a small airport, we keep straight, following a dirt track, and suddenly we're in rainforest. The canopy of soaring palms and massive fruit trees blocks out most of the light as we pick our way over looping vines and fallen logs. We have to detour off the track several times to skirt deep, water-filled trenches, and each time we find our way back, it seems more overgrown. Clearly, it's not a well-traveled route. I ask Zach repeatedly if he's sure we're going the right way as we trudge, swat, hop and duck amid a cacophony of birds and buzzing insects.

Two hours in, I've lost what little faith I had in Zach's map-reading skills. When he informs me we're leaving the track to take a narrow path that is so overgrown I wouldn't have noticed it, I slump down on the nearest log and eye him dubiously.

"You sure about that, buddy?"

"Yeah." He pulls up his shirt and uses the edge of it to wipe the sweat from his face.

I take a swig from my water bottle and look around.

"Can I look at the map?"

He hands it over, and I smooth out the sweat-soaked napkin to see what must be the track we're on because it cuts straight across the island, and, sure enough, there's a dotted line off to the right.

"How do you know this is the right path?" I ask.

Zach opens his bag, pulls out two beers, cracks them open and hands one over. He polishes his off in one go.

"Fourth path," he says, pointing to a four in the corner of the napkin. "Lemon wrote the four to help me remember."

"You were counting paths?" I exclaim, impressed.

Zach returns to rummaging through his bag.

"Zach? Were you counting the paths, buddy?"

He swats a bug-eyed dragonfly that torpedoes into his face and turns away to track the sound of a woodpecker high up in an almond tree. I hunker down and sip my beer.

ME: *Was I ever this irresponsible?*

PAT: *Well, let's see. Even if we only consider last semester, you got high and crashed the family car, beat our school record for the most hours spent in detention and borrowed my iPod without asking and lost it. So what do you think?*

ME: *I didn't lose your stupid iPod.*

PAT: *Really, then where is it?*

ME: *Forget it.*

PAT: *No, tell me, what did you do with it?*

ME: *Do you remember the last time you had it? You asked me to get it from your room so we could listen to a tune you'd just downloaded.*

PAT: *Yeah, I remember. You took it and stormed out of the house.*

ME: *I read the e-mail, Pat, the one from the Shark Center offering you the internship. You left it open on the screen and sent me in there because you wanted me to read it.*

PAT: *So why didn't you say anything?*

ME: *What was there to say? Obviously, you wanted to go.*
PAT: *It was a great opportunity, but with everything that had been happening, I wanted us to talk about it. I wouldn't have sent you in there if I'd already made my decision. And that wasn't the only time I tried to talk to you, Luke. Every time I brought it up, you shut me out.*
ME: *I sold your iPod to buy weed.*
PAT: *Oh, very mature!*
ME:

The first bite feels like the flame of a lighter against my skin, though the only time I've actually had that experience, I'd just knocked back half a bottle of single malt, so this feels ten times worse.

"What the . . .!" I jump up.

Zach pulls me toward him. "Fire ants," he says, pointing to a bunch of innocuous-looking ants marching around the spot I just vacated. "You okay?"

I look at the line of red dots up the back of my calf.

"Yeah," I say. It hurts like hell. "No problem."

"I might have lost track," he says glumly.

"What?" My skin is starting to blister.

"I definitely counted two or three."

I think I'm having an allergic reaction. The throbbing is getting worse.

"There were a couple of things that might have been paths. Not more than five, that's for sure."

I run my fingers over the welts. They feel hot.

"So we better keep moving," says Zach. "It's getting late."

I want to suggest we turn back, but I can't waste another day no closer to finding my sister.

"You don't happen to have a first-aid kit in there?" I ask, following Zach off road. He clambers over the log I was just sitting on, but I hack my way through some bushes to the side of it. I'm not risking any more bites.

"Sorry, no medical kit," he apologizes, "but I've got more beer."

"Maybe later, thanks."

The next hour is hard going. Over and over, we have to take major detours off the path to avoid puddles the size of inland lakes. Two or three times, the path curves so sharply I think we're doubling back, but everything looks alike. I can't tell if we're climbing over the same dead wood, crawling under the same vines and going round the same ponds or if it's all new territory. It doesn't help that the ground is infested with massive ant mounds, which I give a wide berth, while simultaneously trying to avoid the biters on the ground. I spend as much time watching my feet as I do looking ahead, so more than a few times, I get whacked in the face with foliage.

Zach insists on stopping to admire every freaking reptile we come across. I share his excitement over the first few dozen, but after that, every rainbow spotted lizard–iguana–salamander–snake starts to look like so much shoe leather.

"Zach," I say, stopping to consult my watch. "We may have a problem."

He leans against a spindly tree, and I notice for the first time that we're surrounded by spindly trees. When did we leave behind the thick soaring trees of the rainforest? When did the ground change from dry with occasional puddles to damp with occasional dry spots?

"Two problems," I say.

He looks at me apprehensively.

"We've been walking for four hours, more than two on this path, and it's almost six o'clock. That means we have only one more hour of daylight."

"We're almost there," he says, pulling out a pack of smokes and offering me one.

I shake my head. "And secondly, I think we've hit swamp."

"We may have one more problem," he says, taking a long slow drag as he scrutinizes something behind me.

"What?"

"I'm pretty sure that log behind you just moved."

I turn around — slowly. There are more dead leaves and branches on the ground than overhead, but I don't see anything out of the ordinary.

"Looks fine to me."

"Keep watching," he says.

"Oh, shit!"

"Uh-huh."

"Back away slowly," I whisper, keeping myself between Zach and the croc.

I can't tell if it's watching us, but there's something about the way it shifts ever so slightly that gets my heart pounding. We haven't taken more than a few steps before it leaps into action, lifting its body off the ground and galloping toward us. I overtake Zach in seconds and grab his arm, dragging him with me. His pack slips and I snatch it up without breaking stride. We leap logs and branches, sprint through mud that sucks at our feet and dodge trees, hoping something will slow the creature down. We run till we can't run anymore and we don't look back.

Finally, Zach drags on my arm.

"I need to stop, man," he puffs, leaning over with his hands on his thighs.

I look around but can't see any sign of the predator. I don't know if we've lost it or it's lurking in the ooze that is now above our ankles.

"I think it's gone," I say.

"It's not the only thing that's gone." Zach stands up and takes the measure of our surroundings.

"We've lost the path," I say grimly.

He nods.

"And it's getting dark."

There's no sign of the forest now. We're smack in the middle of a mangrove swamp.

"Beer?" he offers, reaching for his pack, which is still slung from my shoulder. I hand it over and he pulls out two beers and a bag of chips.

I'm light-headed with relief at the sight of food, despite the fact we're royally screwed and probably won't survive the night. There's nowhere to sit, so the best we can do is break off a few mangrove branches and make a spiky pile that gets us inches out of the mud. As night falls, bats swoop all around us and the birdsong is replaced by an eerie clacking.

"What is that?" I ask.

"Crabs."

I look around. Sure enough, we're surrounded by heaving masses of crabs scuttling about like armored spiders in the fading light.

"They're not dangerous," says Zach unconvincingly.

"I think we're going to have to stay here till morning." I consider adding that he should have told me when he first realized he might have miscounted the paths. I can't believe I let him get me into this mess and all to get information on voodoo dolls, which I don't even believe in. But as I look at Zach staring at the ground, his shoulders drooping, I just don't have the heart to add to his misery by complaining.

"It's not your fault, Zach."

"I got us lost."

"The croc got us lost."

"I always mess up," he says quietly.

I know the feeling, which makes me determined not to let Zach feel that way. I try to make out his expression in the gloom, but we're sitting awkwardly, side by side, on our twiggy nest and he's pointedly turned away from me.

"It's a nice night," I say, trying to sound cheerful. "It's not so hot now and it's not raining. Things could be a lot worse, Zach. In the morning, we'll figure out where we are and walk out of here. It's no big deal."

He doesn't answer and, if anything, slumps lower onto our twiggy perch.

"How old are you?" Maybe I can take his mind off our situation. I'd been assuming he was Pat's age, but now I'm not so sure.

"Official or real age?"

I smile. "Both."

"My ID says I'm twenty. That's what people here think I am."

"Twenty? They really believe you're twenty?"

"Yeah," he says. "Why wouldn't they?"

"No reason," I say quickly. "It's just, if you were getting a fake ID, I would have thought you might go for something a little younger. Pat says you only need to be eighteen to become a dive master."

"I needed to be eighteen when I was fifteen," he says in a low voice. "I got the fake ID when my mom kicked me out. So now that I'm seventeen, I'm twenty. You get it?"

"I think so," I say. "So you've been on your own for two years?"

He grunts, which I take to mean yes.

"I'm really sorry, man," I say and know exactly how meaningless that sounds because people keep saying it to me.

"It's probably for the best," he says wearily. "My mom went through a lot of boyfriends after my dad left, but they all had one thing in common. They liked to hit. The first time I hit back, she kicked me out, but I was pretty much ready to leave by then anyway. Are your parents still together?"

"That's one way of putting it," I say. "Mom's threatened to leave a couple of times but she never does. Sometimes she gets worked up and says Dad's ruined her life, but only when she's really wasted."

"Your mom gets wasted?" Zach sounds way more disapproving than I would have expected for a guy who considers beer one of the basic food groups.

"My parents were our age when Mom got pregnant. They weren't even dating. Dad was taking photos of my mom for the school paper. She was head cheerleader, and he had this huge nerdy crush on her. I think they only hooked up the one time, but they hit the jackpot. Pat says Mom wishes she'd never had us. There may be some truth to that but it's not that simple. My mom loves us.

"I don't think anyone is thrilled to have a baby when they're still in high school, and she doesn't cope well with her life not working out like she'd hoped, but she can be really thoughtful. Dad's never made much money and Mom's never worked at all, but every year she manages to get us something really special for Christmas. This year she got Pat a top-of-the-line laptop to take to college. I don't know how Mom ever pulled enough money together, but it was the perfect gift at the perfect time. Just when you think she only cares about herself, she does something like that. The drinking's gotten worse over the years, though. She's tried to stop a few times, but she always goes back to it. I think she's just disappointed with herself, and drinking makes her feel better."

I don't say that it does the same for me. Maybe that's why Pat and I take such different views of it. "Pat fights with her all the time. It doesn't help." I pause, take a deep breath and rush on. "Mom tried to kill herself a few weeks before Pat came down here."

"Wow, man, I'm really sorry. That's brutal."

"At first Pat was furious. She acted like Mom did it deliberately to hurt her, which might have been true. It *was* the night of Pat's graduation. It should have been Pat's perfect night, her reward for all her years of hard work and clean living. Pat gave the valedictory address, and Mom was there in the audience, clapping louder than anyone. Then that night she took sleeping pills. She said it was an accident; she was so overexcited by seeing Pat up there on the podium that she couldn't sleep. But we think she took at least a dozen, with her usual booze. It's hard to imagine how that could have been an accident."

"She sounds a bit whack. Did your dad put her in a mental hospital?"

"Nah, she got her stomach pumped and was home in a few days. Nothing was the same after that, though. I'd always told Pat Mom would try to kill herself someday and we needed to be more careful around her. I'm not blaming Pat. Mom made her own decision."

"That's heavy, dude. Is that why Tricia came to Utila, to get away from all the stress?"

I stare at my feet, lifting them just in time to escape a crab scuttling toward my bare toes, claws outstretched. It launches itself up the side of our perch, following my retracting feet. I break off a twig that's been jabbing my butt for the last several minutes and hold it down to the crab to try to distract it. It latches on with a claw that's obviously designed for combat, being at least three times larger than the other.

"Pat needed to get away." I'm glad of the darkness to hide the guilt in my eyes. "But that's all in the past," I continue resolutely. "The important thing is, I'm going to find Pat, and we'll talk this all out and be a family again." I suddenly realize what I've said. "Geez, Zach, I'm sorry. I wasn't thinking."

"It doesn't matter," he says, but when he runs a hand across his eyes, I think he's crying.

"Of course it doesn't matter," I say, clapping him on the back. "Because we're brothers now, right?"

He turns to me, his eyes glistening in the moonlight, and throws both arms around me in a hug that knocks us both into the muck.

"Damn," I mutter.

"AAAAAIIIIEEEEE!" he screams.

We both struggle to get our footing. My heart is pounding again.

"What is it?" I demand.

"Something bit me," he whimpers. "It hurts, man, it really hurts."

He's cradling his mud-covered hand. I try to get a look at it in the moonlight, cursing our lack of planning. Would it have been too much foresight for one of us to bring a flashlight? I can't even tell if he's bleeding. I use the last bit of the water in my water bottle to wash off the mud. I still can't make out a bite mark, but even in the limited light, I can see it's starting to swell.

"It's going to be okay." I hope he can't hear the panic in my voice. There could be any number of poisonous creatures out here, wherever the heck here is. A long way from help, that's for sure.

"I think I'm dying," he wheezes, his breath coming in short gasps.

Holy shit. Holy shit.

"Help!" I shout, sounding every bit like I'm in some cheesy horror flick. "HELP!" I bellow, even though we're in the middle of nowhere and I'm more likely to attract crocs than rescue.

I pull Zach onto our branch nest and put my arm around him, wondering what the hell I'm going to do. If I leave him and go for help, I'll only get myself more lost. And if by some miracle I find my way out of the forest, I doubt I could ever find my way back to Zach. Maybe we should try to walk out together, dark as it is. But what if we just go deeper into the swamp or stumble into another crocodile? Cold beads of sweat pop out on my forehead as I peer into the murky moonlight, where every gnarled tree looks like a monster.

Did something move?

A shape emerges from the darkness.

It steps toward us.

"Zombie," whispers Zach.

I shiver.

CHAPTER 9

"What you boys be doin' out here?" the spectral figure shouts in a very unzombie-like voice.

I stand up, shaky with relief.

"Don't answer," hisses Zach.

"I think she's already spotted us. If it's a zombie, we're dead meat anyway."

"Don't say *dead meat* in front of a Z-O-M-B-Y," Zach whimpers.

"I-E, it's spelled . . . never mind. I'm pretty sure it's not a zombie, Zach. Just wait here."

I attempt to walk over to the figure, but Zach digs his fingers into my arm with a grip that would put any zombie to shame.

"Ow," I say, slogging through the muck, with Zach firmly attached.

It's slow going, but the figure waits patiently.

As we get close, I can see it's a large woman wearing a flouncy skirt, gum boots, a loose T-shirt and a headscarf. Her black skin gleams in the moonlight. If she is a zombie, she's very well turned out.

"Excuse me," I say. "We appear to be lost."

"You don't say."

Just my luck; we get rescued by someone with enough attitude to make me wonder if I should have kept my mouth shut and taken my chances with the crocs.

"We were looking for the home of Martha, the bush doctor."

"It's Miss Martha. Didn't your mama teach you how to speak to a lady?"

"No, mostly she taught me how to hold my liquor."

"That figures. Who told you I was a bush doctor? I don't appreciate bein' called no bush doctor."

"Lemon," I say, giving him up without a moment's hesitation. He's definitely getting spit in his next remedy. "The thing is," I rush on, "my friend's hurt. Something bit him."

Zach's breathing fast and leaning on me like he's having trouble standing up on his own. I put my arm around him. I really hope he doesn't pass out. I'm not sure how far I could carry him.

Martha steps forward and holds out her hand to him. "Where you hurt, child?" she says in a gentle voice.

He whimpers and puts his hand in hers. She reaches her other hand into her voluminous skirt and pulls out a flashlight. When she switches it on, I get a good look at Zach for the first time this evening. His hand is swollen and red, but it's his face, streaked with tears, that makes me turn away. I wish Martha would shut off the goddamn light.

"It's not too serious," she says reassuringly. "Just a scorpion sting. You got a bad reaction is all. It affects some worse than others. Come on home and I'll fix you."

Martha leads the way, and Zach and I trudge behind her. He's still leaning heavily on me, my arm hooked under his shoulder. He slips in the mud a few times, and we both nearly go down. I just manage to keep us upright. Finally, we're on drier ground, though the going doesn't get much easier in the inky shadows cast by the looming trees.

Martha sings as we walk along. Zach's breathing slows to the rhythm of her music so I'm grateful. The sweat is rolling off me in sheets by the time we reach a clearing with a single thatch-roofed house on stilts. It's a long way from where we started. I wonder how Martha could possibly have heard me shouting from this far away. Even stranger, how could she have reached us so fast? An icicle of fear invades my thoughts.

Me: *I think she's a witch.*

Pat: *What are you doing here? I thought you were looking for me?*

Me: *I'm following a lead. Tracy said you had a doll under your step the day before you disappeared, and then I got one, too. It's not like it's just a greeting card, Pat. Someone must be trying to scare us, if not harm us.*

Pat: *So you think this witch is going to tell you who's planting the dolls?*

Me: *She's bound to know who else on the island is into voodoo.*

Pat: *But if she really is a witch, how can she be trusted?*

Me: *What choice do I have? Anyway, you always said I should be open to new experiences.*

Pat: *I meant diving, you moron.*

Me:

We climb up to her veranda and pass through her screened front door. I'm careful not to let my hand disturb the three large spiders that cling to it. A cockroach scuttles out of our path as we enter. There's a single kerosene lantern sitting on a table in the middle of the room, a cot in one murky corner and a stove and sink along one wall. Despite the large screened windows on all sides, the still air hangs fetid, rank with the smell of fish and overripe fruit.

Geckos chirp from the walls at the edges of the lamp glow, darting forward every few seconds to catch flying insects, the tiny biters that have been feasting on me since I got to this island. I realize I must have sweated off the bug spray as I feel them start to nip. Along two sides of the room are rows of shelves packed with jars of various sizes. It's too dark to see what's in them, but they dominate the space like living things lying in wait.

"Sit him down there," orders Martha. I lead Zach over to one of the chairs next to the table. I have to pry his fingers off before easing him down. His face is gray under his pink, peeling flesh, and he immediately puts his head down on folded arms.

"He needs anti-venom," I say urgently, forgetting I'm nervous of this woman and not sure I trust her.

"That so?" Martha glances at me from a stool she's climbed up on to lift down jars. "You an expert on scorpion bites?"

I walk over to her and take the jars she hands down to me, setting them on the counter. "Maybe he's allergic," I say in a low voice, looking back at Zach to make sure he hasn't heard. He doesn't stir at all, which is even worse. I almost wish he'd start crying again. At least then I'd know he was conscious.

"Why don't you make yourself useful and start the water to boiling," says Miss Martha, not unkindly. "I need two pots, 'bout a cup in each." She gestures at the stove.

I look around for matches to light the gas. I'm pleased and surprised when I notice a modern flint lighter hanging on a hook just beside the stove. Of course, by "modern" I mean invented in the past one hundred years. I get the burners going on the first try, fill the two pots and set them on the flames.

Miss Martha's busy taking out leaves and seeds from the jars. I cast furtive glances at her, both creeped out and fascinated. She dumps the seeds straight into two wooden bowls, but she chops the leaves first, separating them into piles before she adds different combinations to the seeds. Then she takes a small stone pestle and begins grinding. Her large body casts huge shadows on the wall, making her seem even more witchlike. The jars don't have labels, but she scooped out the ingredients without hesitation. She keeps singing a haunting song. This time I know she's not singing to us.

"Water's boiling," I say.

I wonder how far I could carry Zach if I had to get him to town for proper medical treatment. I'm tired and weak with hunger. Other than the half bag of chips, I haven't eaten since breakfast, at least twelve hours ago. Zach's a scrawny guy, though. I might be able to carry him a couple of miles. The problem is, we walked a lot farther than a couple of miles to get here. As usual, my sister is right. Coming out here was a spectacularly dumb-ass idea.

Martha shuffles over, nudges me out of the way and dumps a different concoction into each pot. She reaches up and takes down two wooden spoons that were hanging from nails above the range.

"Stir," she orders and hands me the spoons. "And don't be lettin' them burn, you hear?"

"Right," I say, glad to have something to do. I look worriedly over at Zach, who's still not moving.

She runs a cloth under the tap, walks over to him and cleans the area around the bite. Zach winces and makes a small noise. Martha keeps singing away in a language I've never heard before. I really hope it's not some crazy witch incantation.

The dried foliage in my pots is softening; one has turned soupy green, like pond scum, while the other thickens into a paste that quickly becomes impossible to stir. I lift it off the heat and set it on the counter.

"I think this one's ready," I say, expecting another snarky remark, but Martha's way too busy with her freaky singing, which now sounds more like chanting.

She comes over and looks in the pots, quietly humming now. Taking a mug down from a shelf, she lifts the second pot off the stove and pours the soupy mixture into it.

Holy shit, she's going to make him drink it. What did she put in there? I should have been paying attention. What if it's poison? But why would she poison him?

"We need to let them cool a spell," she says. "You hungry?"

My stomach growls at the mention of food, but I eye the fungus soup.

"No," I say, "I'm good."

She snorts. "When you be a guest in my house, you gonna eat," she insists. "So sit your backside down in that chair and don't you be forgettin' to say grace."

I've never said grace in my life, but it seems like a good sign that she wants me to call on the guy up there and not the other one, so I sit down and give it a try.

"Hey, God," I say, keeping my voice friendly, though He's never played a big role in my life up to now, and given the way things have been going lately, I don't think I'm on His Christmas card list either. "I just want You to know that if You had anything to do with getting us lost, I'm cool with that. Even siccing the croc on us was okay, since we got away and all, but my sister disappearing and the scorpion biting Zach were really overkill. If You were trying to make some kind of point . . ."

"What in all creation are you goin' on about?" Martha cuts off my dialogue with the Almighty as if it wasn't her idea in the first place.

I eyeball her. She is one hard witch to please.

She stalks over carrying a steaming pot and wielding a large metal ladle like it's her weapon of choice.

"Sorry," I say. "I was just, you know, praying. . . ."

"You call that prayin'?" She slams the pot down on the table. "When you address your Lord, you use respect, boy. And you thank Him. You don't be tellin' Him what He did wrong, and you sure don't be blamin' Him for you gettin' you'self lost in the swamp. That wasn't His idea."

I'm on the point of arguing, but the smell coming out of the pot starts wafting in my direction and my mouth waters so much I'm practically drooling.

"Thanks, God," I say hurriedly. "Can I eat now?"

Martha snorts again, but she goes back to the kitchen area and fetches bowls. She spoons out two heaping portions and slides one in front of Zach. He doesn't move at all, so I lean over to him and listen. His breathing is deep and regular. Would he still be breathing if he'd gone into anaphylactic shock? With a pang of guilt, I dig into the stew and with even more guilt, I actually enjoy it. It may be the best food I've ever tasted. I can't shovel it in fast enough, and my bowl is empty in seconds. I run my finger around the surface, mopping up the dregs.

Martha comes back to the table with the paste and begins rubbing it on Zach's hand. That gets his attention. His eyes fly open and he sits bolt upright.

"It stings," he moans.

"Go get him the tea," she says to me.

I leap to do the witch's bidding.

She holds the mug to his lips. I'm stunned when he greedily downs the vile brew without a murmur.

"Try your stew, buddy," I say. "It's really good." And might even get rid of the disgusting tea taste. The smell alone is making me gag.

Zach drops his head back on the table and closes his eyes again. Martha bustles around her kitchen, tidying up. I keep one eye on her as I slide Zach's bowl over and start slurping up his share.

"I see you be likin' my boil-up," she says, still with her back to me as she washes pots at the sink.

Definitely a witch. She has eyes in the back of her freaking head. I wonder again how she knew Zach and I were out in the swamp. Was she following us?

"The spirits," she says, startling me out of my thoughts.

"What?"

"You be wonderin' how I knew you were in trouble. The spirits be tellin' me."

I slurp Zach's stew and ignore her. If she's messing with me, I'm not rising to it, and if she isn't . . . well, I don't even want to think about that possibility.

"You ever talk to spirits?" she asks, turning to me. Her features are concealed in the dim light of the kerosene lantern. Only her eyes shine out from the gloom.

"No, never."

She's probably crazy. It would explain why she's living way out here on her own.

"You sure about that?" She steps forward into the light, and I feel like she's looking right inside of me. I stare down at the empty bowl and wish I hadn't eaten so much as my stomach twists with anxiety.

"Why'd you come all the way out here to see me?"

"You mean your spirits didn't tell you?" I quip, before it occurs to me I probably don't want to get her angry.

"What do *your* spirits tell *you*?" she asks in a voice that echoes in the stillness of the night.

"I don't know what you're talking about," I say, though of course I do know, but how does she? I stand up and walk to the door. The three spiders are still there, probably her pets. I tap the screen and watch them converge in excitement.

"The spirit doesn't depart when the body does. It needs time to get used to the idea of bein' dead. Sometimes it's got unfinished business. It might hang round for a year or more before it be ready to make the journey across the sea."

The spiders retreat to their outposts again, a circle of death waiting for the unwary to step among them.

"We gather the family, pray for its journey and bathe its spirit to help it prepare."

I wonder why the spiders stay together. Are they a family? Siblings, maybe?

"But the ancestors don't ever leave completely. You can always call 'em back when you need 'em."

Or are they like sharks, cooperating in the hunt until one of their own shows weakness and becomes the victim?

"Love doesn't die with the body."

"I hear my sister's voice in my head, but she's not dead."

A chair crashes to the floor, and I whip round to see Zach, standing strong, staring at me.

"Tricia talks to you?" he croaks.

"Yeah," I admit, torn between a reluctance to share this with him and overwhelming relief that he's okay. Now that I've admitted it out loud, it sounds ridiculous. I expect him to challenge me or even scoff.

"Does she talk about me?" he asks, hope so plain on his face, it might as well be written in Magic Marker.

I hesitate. It wasn't the response I was expecting. I'm not sure I'm even happy he believes me if it's going to lead to a whole lot of questions.

ME: *You got any words of wisdom here, Sis?*

PAT: *Just tell him I think about him all the time.*

"You're always on her mind," I say.

PAT: *That's not quite what I said.*

"What does she say?" he asks excitedly.

ME: *Well?*

PAT: *He's a good friend.*

"You're her best friend."

"I knew it," Zach crows.

He really *is* feeling better.

"Luke, I need you to ask her something," says Zach, suddenly serious.

"Yeah?"

"I always wanted to ask her out, but I never thought she'd go for a guy like me. Could you ask her if I ever had a chance?"

"I think she has a boyfriend, buddy. Remember Jamie, your friend?"

I glance at Martha, who's leaning on the kitchen counter, a bemused look on her face.

"I never heard of no courtin' the dead," she says.

"She's not dead," I remind her irritably.

"Just ask her, man. I know it's not likely, but the thing is, besides you, she's the only person who never made me feel like a loser, and maybe if a girl like her could see something in me . . ." His eyes mist over.

"Okay, I'll ask."

"Wait," he says urgently. He licks his hand and does his best to smooth down his hair, which is shooting up on one side from where he slept on it. Then he ducks his head and not so surreptitiously sniffs his pits. He straightens up, looking glum. "Okay, go ahead," he says, folding his arms across his chest.

ME: *Well, Pat?*

PAT: *Do you think he might have brain damage?*

I smile at Zach. "She can't wait to date you, man."

PAT: *You are such an asshole.*

"Tell her I love her," Zach gushes.

PAT: *Tell him he's supposed to breathe in the oxygen when he's diving.*

"She loves you too, buddy."

Zach rights his chair and sinks down into it, overcome with emotion.

PAT: *Are you planning to fix this?*

ME: *You want it fixed, then get back here and fix it yourself.*

"I always knew we had this special bond," murmurs Zach. "It's like you and me, we're connected." His eyes burn into me, and I wonder if maybe he's still running a fever. I walk over and put my hand on his forehead. It feels hot, but when I put my hand on my own forehead, it feels the same. Not surprising, since the room's a sauna. I sit down in the chair opposite, and Martha comes over with a fresh bowl and dishes him out some stew.

"You want more?" she asks me.

I shake my head.

"I've been thinking," says Zach. "Maybe we're descended from the same Mayan family, and we ended up all over America but we were drawn back here because this is where we all started."

"Weren't no Mayans on Utila," says Martha. "You coulda been Paya Indian, though. Can't dig a ditch here without disturbin' a Payan grave."

"I don't think we look much like Indian descendants," I point out.

"We must be reincarnated," Zach exclaims excitedly. "That would totally explain everything."

I'm happy he's feeling better, but I'm ready to drop from exhaustion and I've had enough of this spooky lady and her spirit-infested house. We need to get down to business and get out of here.

"We wanted to ask you about this," I say, pulling the doll out of my pocket and placing it on the table.

Zach jerks his chair back but leans in to get his bowl, keeping his eyes on the doll the whole time. Martha also stays well back from the doll. It lies there in the eerie lamp glow, sodden from our plunge in the swamp, its black hair muddy and matted. One eye is gone where the stitching has started to fray. As I look at it, my chest starts to ache; sadness overwhelms me, and I get a flash of something. At first it hovers just on the edge of my consciousness, like a forgotten memory, but as the light flickers across the bedraggled doll, the image crystallizes, emerging from the deep recesses of my mind. I'm no longer looking at the doll but at my sister.

It's her hair, wet and matted but with blood and small white shards in it — bone from her shattered skull. And her eye, like the doll's, is missing, gouged out, leaving only a gaping hole. Her shirt is ripped and twisted, exposing bare flesh, and her body sways as if it has life, but there's no life in the one remaining eye that glares accusingly from her pallid, bloated face.

My stomach roils and my legs tremble as I stumble to my feet and dash for the door. I push through it, hitting the railing with a thump, and lean over, my breath coming in short bursts, stew churning inside the burning cauldron of my belly. The ground below blurs as my eyes fill with tears. It's a relief when I finally start to vomit. Every spoonful of Martha's stew plummets over the side of her deck, until I'm empty. Still my stomach lurches and twists as if it could expel not just the contents of my body but every thought and memory from my entire screwed-up life.

I don't realize Martha has followed me till I feel her hand on my shoulder. "Come inside, child. I'll fix you some tea."

She holds the door for me as I stagger back to my chair. Martha busies herself in the kitchen while Zach slurps his stew, trying to keep an eye on me and the doll at the same time. I stare at the floor and take deep breaths, still trembling with the horror I now feel for the doll. My heart throbs in my ears as I struggle to vanquish the images of my sister bombarding my mind. It's a living nightmare. I know it can't be true. But where did it come from?

"It makes me feel sick, too, man," Zach says, polishing off his bowl and standing up to help himself to some more.

I stare at him in shock. Did he see Pat as well? But he nods in the direction of the doll.

"It looks like a puchinga doll," says Martha from the other side of the kitchen, where she's cutting leaves for my tea.

I put my head in my hands and close my eyes, trying to replace the horrible image of Pat with the one that usually comes to mind when I think of her — green eyes that darken when she's angry, her teasing smile that always makes me feel no problem is as bad as it seems.

ME: *You are alive, aren't you, Pat? That was just my imagination, right?*

I listen for her voice but it's strangely silent.

"I've heard tell there's some who be practicin' the old ways," says Martha. "Where'd you find it?"

I take a minute to realize she's still talking about the doll.

She puts my tea on to boil and returns to the table, circles the doll twice, examining it from all angles.

"It was under my doorstep." I take a shaky breath. "A girl told me my sister found one under her step just before she disappeared." It sounds silly when I say it out loud, but Martha's not laughing.

"Is he cursed?" asks Zach, still wolfing down stew.

"Could be," says Martha.

Zach and I look at each other. His eyes are round with fear. I struggle to keep my own fear in check. Just because Martha believes in voodoo magic doesn't make it real.

"My people aren't no witches," says Martha, setting a cup of tea down in front of me.

I sniff it. It smells pretty good so I take a sip. It tastes even better than it smells.

"Doesn't mean there aren't no witches around," she continues. "There always be some who prefer evil when they could as easily do good. You got any idea who might want to harm you?"

I shake my head.

"The same person who took Tricia," says Zach. "That's his sister.

"And my girlfriend," he adds.

I choke on my tea and start coughing.

Martha stands up to pat me on the back. "I can help you," she says. "How much money you boys got?"

This starts a whole new coughing fit. Zach immediately pulls a soaking wad of cash out of his pocket and plops it on the table. He's already produced more than I want to spend on what's probably a scam, and I start calculating how much I can afford to repay him from my meager funds.

Martha picks up the money and it vanishes into her skirt. She looks at me for a moment, but I just take another sip of my tea and don't meet her eyes. She huffs a little before going over to her footstool and pulling down jars again. Zach plays witch's apprentice this time, while I watch in silence.

"Witchcraft be practiced all over the Caribbean," says Martha, "but the Garifuna, my people, we aren't climbin' into that crazy boat."

So Martha doesn't believe in witchcraft either. This is the best news I've heard all night.

"The Good Lord doesn't hold with no witchcraft," she continues. "It's not Christian, if ya get what I'm sayin'."

I'm not sure I'm on board with the God stuff, but I can set that aside for a fellow skeptic.

"There be angry souls among the dead."

She's lost me.

"We don't be callin' on their sort." She starts boiling another brew. "But that doesn't mean we won't try to make peace with them."

I'd really like to know how much Zach paid for us to appease people who can't hold their temper, even when they're six feet under.

Martha starts her spooky singing again as she mixes the new potion. I notice there's a pattern to it. She pauses every once in a while like she's giving someone else a chance to respond. Zach and I don't speak Crazy, so no one answers. In fact, the way she cocks her head like she's listening, I'm not so sure she isn't hearing a response.

Pat: *Is that so hard to believe?*

I'm so relieved to hear Pat's voice that I have to bite my lip to keep from grinning, but I play it cool. I don't want her thinking I expected anything less.

ME: *What? You're on the witch's side now?*

PAT: *She fixed Zach.*

ME: *I thought you were the scientist.*

PAT: *I am. And you're the one who talks to someone who isn't there.*

ME:

Martha comes over and puts her pot down on the table.

"What's your name, child?"

"Luke."

She sticks her finger in the pot, then smears her mixture on my forehead. I can feel her making the shape of the cross. She chants the whole time, her voice wheedling. My name keeps coming up. I wonder what flattery she's laying out, whose favor she's trying to secure to protect me. The ceremony, if you can call it that, lasts only a few minutes. As she resumes her seat, the paste hardens on my skin, pulling my flesh tight around it. It feels itchy and I want to rub it off, but instead I stand up.

"We should be getting back," I say.

"It won't be light for an hour," she says.

Zach shoots me a nervous look.

"It's a long walk," I say firmly. "We need to get started."

Zach sighs, then gets to his feet and Martha with him.

"I'll set you on the right road," she says, "and give you my flashlight."

"We can't take that," I say. Despite our recent cash infusion, this woman doesn't have enough to be giving things away.

"It's just a loan," she says, fixing me with a knowing look. "Something tells me you're going to be around awhile. We might even make a Utilan out of you. Just remember, child, the spirits are always there when you really need them, but there will come a time when you need to let them go."

CHAPTER 10

I say almost nothing on the long five-hour hike home. We emerge from the forest much closer to town than I expected, which means we must have overshot the path the first time. Zach and I part ways at Bluewater, and I head back to the Shark Center alone. I turned down his suggestion we get breakfast and he didn't push it. He was gleeful about our success in finding Martha and enlisting her help. I didn't have the heart to tell him I think it's a load of bull. I rubbed off most of the voodoo protection before we even left the woods. Uppermost in my mind is that we just wasted almost twenty-four hours. It's the start of my third day in Utila, and I'm more confused about Pat's disappearance than when I arrived. I didn't expect she'd be easy to find, but I certainly didn't expect she'd been targeted by someone practicing voodoo, and I'm still unsettled by her apparent personality transformation and secret boyfriend.

The hike back has sapped every ounce of my energy and I'm drenched in sweat, which seems to be my usual condition in this place. I'm not going to be able to think straight until I get a shower and some alone-time, so when a total stranger rushes purposefully out of an open doorway and plants himself in my path, I simply swerve sideways to avoid a collision.

Unfortunately, as I jog right so does he, and when I shift left, he's there as well. Standing still in frustration, I give him a bleary stare and take a startled step backward from the force of hostility in his bloodshot eyes.

"You got a problem?" I ask.

"I got a message for your sister," he snarls, closing the six inches of space between us and shoving me backward. I hold my ground but begin to regret it as the reek of sweat and stale beer radiates off him.

I stare as he twitches in front of me like he's got invisible bugs skittering across his flesh. Long fraying dreads, thin ropy body, corroded teeth — the guy's obviously been downing a lot more than beer on a regular basis.

"You may not have heard," I say, deciding to take a conciliatory approach. No point antagonizing a guy who's got this much junk in him. "My sister has been missing for almost two weeks."

"Are you makin' fun of me, boy?"

I sigh, shift my weight and wonder how hard it would be to just knock him over and keep going. Shopkeepers are starting to appear, unlocking doors and sweeping the street in front of their shops. Is it my imagination or are they all pointedly ignoring us?

"I know ya sister be hidin'."

"Excuse me?" My attention snaps back to the crackhead in front of me.

"She knows what's good for 'er."

"Are you threatening my sister?" I ask, still more confused than upset.

"Just saying what's true is all. Ain't no threat. Bobby gonna mess with her bad if she come back 'ere. Ya tell her dat. Ya tell her she bes' stay missin'."

I'm shaking from the charge of blood coursing through me as I struggle to keep my voice even. Is it possible I've finally stumbled across the person responsible for Pat's disappearance? "What do you know about my sister?"

"Why don't ya ask her?" he says, but I can see the thought dawning on him that maybe I really don't know where she is. A smile creeps across his face and that's when I lose it.

I'm on him before I realize it's happening. The first punch connects with his rotting teeth, and I think I feel one crumble beneath my fist. He goes down fast, but I don't have time to feel victory or even remorse as heavy hands claw at my back, pulling me up and hurling me across the street. I hit a storefront, stagger, then turn to take a full-frontal blow to the face. Stumbling backwards, I go down on one knee and am up again fast, just in time to take another couple of punches, first to my jaw and then to my stomach. As I hit the pavement, I see the crackhead is still lying in the dust where I left him. Looking up to see who's pulverizing me, I see a boot coming for my head. I roll away and up onto my hands and knees, scrabbling sideways, trying to get on my feet before my attacker can finish me off.

A part of my brain registers shock. Who are these people? How can this be happening? But a greater part of me feels only fury. I've been wanting to hit someone from the time I heard Pat was missing. I launch myself at the hulking Rasta, twice my size, and don't even consider the consequences.

He catches me in midair and half-carries, half-drags me through an open doorway. I realize it's the door these guys emerged from. I'm struggling, pummeling him, trying to break free, but it's like he doesn't feel it. I'm dimly aware we're passing some half-empty tables. It's some kind of bar, and there're guys still drinking, though the sun's well up. The only light is the wan beam filtering in from the door we just entered and a few slivers from some shuttered windows. There are a few glances our way as I'm frog-marched past, but I know none of these guys is going to help me. I stop struggling and just focus on staying upright as I'm shoved through another open door. I whip around as the door slams shut behind me and I'm in midair, hurling myself at it, when I hear a bolt slide into place.

I'm alone, in absolute darkness. I bang furiously on the door. "Let me out!" I scream. "Open the frigging door! Are you crazy? Let me out of here right now! Goddamnit!"

I hurl myself at the door, which barely shakes under the impact. Finally, I slump to the floor, pulling up my knees and resting my head on my folded arms.

"What did you get yourself into, Pat?" I ask out loud.

I jump as I hear a noise in the corner. For a brief second I imagine I've finally found her, but when the noise comes again I realize it's just some rodent scurrying around.

"Who are these people? What did you do to piss them off?"

I peer into the darkness and slowly it seems to lighten. Just a few feet in front of me is a circle of radiance, and right in the center of it is my sister — not the Pat of my nightmares or the party girl I never knew, but Pat the way I've seen her a thousand times, sitting cross-legged on the floor, her face buried in a book. She's so close, I could reach out and touch her. My breath catches in my throat and I hold it, frightened I'll startle her, scare her away. She glances up and smiles, as if amused by my nervousness, and returns her attention to the book. I hear the soft rustle of a page when she flips it. It occurs to me I haven't slept in more than twenty-four hours. I'm probably dehydrated, and the blow I took to the head may be more serious than I thought, but if this is a hallucination, I don't want it to end. I stay very still and watch her breathe.

She turns another page.

Lifting a lock of her hair, she absentmindedly winds it around her index finger, the way she always did when she was engrossed in something.

Her clear green eyes move back and forth along the lines. Her forehead puckers as she absorbs some random fact that she'll sock away like a castaway hoarding supplies.

She flips another page and looks up, as if checking I'm still there. Then she shifts the book and turns it so I can see the page with her. The caption is too small for me to read, but the vivid photo of an undulating constellation gliding through its azure home is all too familiar.

An eagle ray.

I wonder if she's reopening our argument of the previous day. I'm prepared to agree that this creature is as beautiful as it is dangerous if Pat will only agree not to disappear again.

Recoiling in shock when the door rattles behind me, I scramble away before realizing I've blundered into the space that my sister so recently inhabited. My carelessness has extinguished her luminosity. I sense her absence as keenly as I felt her presence just moments ago.

"Pat," I whisper desperately, trying to block out the snick of the bolt being slid across. I blink as light floods the room.

Now I can see I'm in a large storage room, a few cases of beer piled in one corner.

I'm crazy. That's the only explanation. It's one thing to make up conversations with my sister, and if I'm going to be totally honest with myself, it's been a long time since those felt made up. But seeing her? I'm taking crazy to a whole new level. I should go back and move in with Martha.

I rise slowly and turn to the open doorway. Whatever or whoever is going to come through it, this is real.

Suddenly Dr. Jake rushes forward and pulls me into a bear hug. I'm not sure who I expected, but it wasn't him.

"Damn it, mate, you had us all half-dead with fright." He stands back, still clutching me with one hand, and puts the other up to my jaw. "He really knocked you about, didn't he? But not to worry, you're still in one piece. I thought a croc might have got you, so you're looking a damn sight better than I feared. What were you doing going into the swamp at night? And then you come back and get into a row with Bobby's boy." He shakes his head at my colossal lack of judgment. "Were you trying to get yourself killed?"

I don't know what to say. He thinks he's talking to a rational person. Wandering in a swamp and starting a fistfight are the least of my lapses from sane behavior.

"Let's get you home, then," says Dr. Jake, realizing he's not going to get anything intelligent out of me.

Bobby is standing in the doorway to the storage room and steps aside as Jake propels me through, one hand still firmly on my shoulder.

"He started it," Bobby grumbles, but he looks away sheepishly when Dr. Jake holds up his hand for silence.

"I don't want to hear it, Bobby," Jake says. "Count yourself lucky I didn't bring the police with me. You can be dead certain I will rain all bloody hell down on you if you or your boys go near Luke again."

I stop just as we reach the door.

"Wait," I say to Dr. Jake and turn back to Bobby. "What's your problem with my sister?"

Bobby glowers at me.

"The boy asked you a question, Bobby," prompts Dr. Jake. "Do you want to answer him or would you rather answer the police?"

"Ain't no business of yours, Jake," Bobby snarls, but when neither of us moves to leave, he continues, "Dat girl be bad for business, always saying she's gonna put a stop to my activities. Ain't none of her business. But it weren't me that done her in, if that be her fate. You should ask dem who be dropping the cargo. It weren't me responsible for killin' all dem fish."

I look at Dr. Jake to see if he has a clue what this guy's talking about. To my surprise, he nods.

"She was upset about the drug drops," Dr. Jake says. "Let's go, Luke. We can talk on the way home."

I scowl at Bobby. "If I find you have anything to do with my sister's disappearance, I'll be back," I promise fiercely as I follow Dr. Jake outside to the street.

It's blistering hot, and I wince as every inch of my body objects to the simple act of walking. My hand goes to my bruised stomach. I wonder if Dr. Jake's right about no serious damage. He's only a fish doctor, after all.

"What was he talking about back there?" I ask, though it actually hurts to talk.

"There was some trouble a few weeks back. A Venezuelan plane dumped some fuel drums and a huge stash of cocaine in the ocean just offshore, then crash-landed on the island. There'd been talk for a long time that traffickers were stopping off up at the airport to refuel in the middle of the night, but that was the first real proof."

"What did that have to do with my sister?"

"I hope nothing, but she was mighty upset about it. She said something about organizing a meeting to demand an investigation. No one was ever caught, you see."

"I do see," I say, because this is the sister I know all too well — anti-drug, anti-crime, anti-anything that threatens her precious fish, and completely unable to keep her mouth shut.

Me: *Is that it, Pat? You couldn't be satisfied just bossing me around. You had to take on South American drug traffickers?*
Pat: *Well, they couldn't have been any more stubborn than you.*

"Do you think they did something to her?"

"As far as I know, there haven't been any reports of planes landing since the crash, but she did disappear about the same time, now that you mention it." He gives me a troubled look.

Any further speculation is short-circuited by Tracy barreling out of the Shark Center, which we've just reached, and flinging herself on me.

"Thank God you're okay," she squeals, clutching me to her breast. "We were all so worried. Dr. Jake sent out an all-points on the radio, asking if anyone knew where you were. Lemon Larry got back to him and said you might have gone out to old Martha's, but when you weren't back by this morning, we didn't know what to think."

"Radio?" I ask, as I determinedly pull away from her.

"The shortwave radio," Dr. Jake explains. "Everyone on the island has one, every boat as well. It's how we keep track of each other. Except Martha, of course. She says it interferes with her spirits, or some such nonsense."

"Dr. Jake was on it all night," continues Tracy. "We kept Station Sixteen open just for updates on you, but the last anyone saw, you were heading down the road past the airport."

I didn't even notice anyone around when we were passing the airport. It must be a bitch to cut school in this town.

"Sorry to scare you. We got lost and didn't get there until after nightfall. Then we had something to eat and a bit of a rest before heading back." I don't bother filling him in on the voodoo stuff. In the clear light of day, I'm embarrassed that we went all that way for such a stupid reason and have nothing to show for it.

"Well, at least that was a good decision." Dr. Jake gives me a stern look, reminding me it was one of too few in his book. "I expect you're wanting some sleep now."

I nod, though the truth is, there's one thing that I hope will be worth following up on.

"Is Pete around?" I ask.

"He's in the equipment shack," says Dr. Jake. "Is there something I can help you with?"

"No, I just need to ask him something."

"All right, then. I better get on the radio and let everyone know you've returned safely." He ducks into the office, with Tracy close on his heels, while I head to the shack.

Pete is crouched on the floor sorting flippers into sizes and separating them into neat rows. It doesn't look like he lost too much sleep over my disappearance.

"You're back," he says, barely glancing up from his task.

"I was wondering if I could ask you a few more questions about my sister." I'm careful to keep my voice neutral.

Pete immediately stops what he's doing and stands up, looking at me sharply. "I thought we'd covered that," he says.

"Yeah, but you seemed a little unclear on the details before. You weren't sure if you were speaking to Pat that night. Anything more come back to you?"

"No, just what I told you." He folds his arms over his chest.

"You see, that's strange, because someone saw you talking to my sister for a long time. In fact, she says it looked like you were hitting on her."

"So I hit on her. So what? It doesn't mean I had anything to do with her disappearance. She was by herself when she left."

I perk up, suddenly alert.

"You saw her leave?"

"I didn't say that." He leans over and picks up half a dozen weighted belts. Turning his back on me, he starts pulling out weights and piling them on a shelf.

"That's exactly what you said." I step between him and the shelf.

"Okay, so I saw her leave." He glares defiantly. "What difference does it make? She was alone. I don't know what happened to her. Is that clear enough for you?"

My breath is coming in short bursts as adrenaline courses through my body. I've just caught him in a lie, and I'd be willing to bet it isn't his only one. I'd like to beat the truth out of him, but I've already started one fight today and look where that got me, not to mention the fact that he's right. Seeing her walk off on her own, even hitting on her, doesn't prove a thing. No one saw him leave with her.

"You know, if I find out you're lying to me, you're going to regret it." My voice shakes with the effort of holding myself back.

"Whatever." He makes a show of smirking but doesn't quite pull it off. Stepping around me, he goes back to stacking weights.

I stomp to my room, trying to tell myself I'm overreacting. If hitting on my sister were a crime, half the guys in my high school would be locked up. From what I've learned over the last few hours, Pat was on the wrong side of far more dangerous people than this poser. He may not have had anything at all to do with her disappearance. But why is it that every time I get near him, I get a churning in my gut? And it's not my imagination that he's equally twitchy around me.

ME: *I need some guidance here, Pat.*

PAT: *If he walks like a sleazoid and he talks like a sleazoid . . .*

ME: *So he does know something?*

PAT: *You're the one playing detective. You tell me.*

ME:

CHAPTER 11

The pounding starts in my dream, with images of Pat's body crashing against a wooden post. Blood streams from her head. She's struggling with something but doesn't try to save herself as her body cracks against the wood again. I shout at her to watch out. The post is behind her, approaching fast. Why doesn't she see it coming? But she can't hear me over the sound of her own screams. There's another noise, a sound so familiar it's like breathing. But what is it? I wake up in a cold sweat and take a minute to realize the pounding is real.

I'm in my darkened bedroom at the Shark Center, which means I've slept the whole day away. Someone is banging on the door. I get unsteadily to my feet as the sound reverberates through my body, my head throbbing right along with it. I had my alarm set for midafternoon, so I must have slept through it. That sucks. I wanted to talk to Jamie today. I still haven't heard his side of the story about the fight he had with Pat the night she disappeared. Even if that leads nowhere, I need to ask him how far Pat got with her drug investigation. How many people could she have antagonized who might want revenge? I reach for my watch and see it's past nine; maybe not too late to see him if I leave immediately. I grab my shirt as I unlock the door.

Tracy bursts in, tears streaming down her face. It takes a few minutes before I can make any sense of her garbled sobs, since she's thrown herself on my bed and buried her face in my pillow.

"I'm next, I'm next," she blubbers hysterically.

I sigh and sit on the edge of the bed, leaving the door open. "Is there a problem?"

She pops up and throws her arms around me, giving a few last hiccuping moans before she's ready to explain.

"You have to come see," she says, standing up and attempting to pull me to my feet, which doesn't work because I outweigh her by a good forty pounds and I don't want to go anywhere with her.

"See what?" I start massaging my temples. I could sell tickets to the drumming in my head. Maybe I shouldn't have rubbed off the voodoo protection. Or maybe it's the cause.

"The doll," she says, yanking on my arm again. "Hurry, Luke, you have to come."

Of course, I don't have to come at all, and if we're talking about another doll, I definitely don't have to hurry. It's not like it's going to walk off on its own.

She plops back down on my bed and looks at me mournfully.

On the other hand, the only way to get her out of my room is to go with her. I don't know why this girl irritates me so much. Sure she's a flake, but I've met other girls like that who don't usually bother me. Sometimes they're even cute. Also, she was Pat's roommate and supposedly her friend. It's probably just the awkwardness of our last encounter, coupled with the comments she made about Pat, which still rankle. Whatever it is, I want to get rid of her. I jump decisively to my feet.

"You're right, we should hurry."

She eyes me suspiciously but gets up and follows me outside and down the path to her room. She points to her front step, standing well back, and like last time, I'm the one to reach under and drag it out. I have to admit it bears an uncanny resemblance to her, right down to the blond pigtails and blue eyes.

"Are you missing any hair?" I ask, holding it up next to her head so I can compare.

She shrinks back and stares at me in horror.

It seemed like a fair question, but I drop the doll to my side, curling it into my fist so it's out of her sight. Now that I'm up, I'm even more anxious to make a quick exit. I'm certain I'm not going to find any clues to my sister's disappearance here, and I've already wasted the better part of a day and night on one voodoo doll. I refuse to waste time on another.

"You have to check my room for me. I can't go in there alone." She flaps the bottom of her shirt, twisting it up like an anxious six-year-old.

"I have some things I need to do, Tracy."

"I'm scared."

"I promised Zach I'd meet him."

"Just till I fall asleep."

She stares at me with her enormous blue eyes and as certain as doping in the Major Leagues, I know she's playing me. I'm powerless to resist. It's as if my rescue-reflex, in response to her lame rendition of chick-in-distress, is hard-wired into my DNA. I'd really like to know where girls learn to pull this shit and why no one is teaching guys how to deal with it. Girls already have tits. How many more advantages do they need?

"Just for a few minutes," I grumble and follow her inside.

She lies down on her bed, which is either proof of good faith or the next step in her campaign to take me down. I sit on the other bed, realize it must be my sister's and spring up like it's on fire. Walking over to the desk, I sit there and stare out the window.

"Who do you think is doing this?" Tracy asks.

I'm so preoccupied, trying to figure out her endgame, that it takes me a minute to understand what she's talking about.

"Don't know."

"Do you think it's Reesie? She hangs around here all the time."

I cut her a look. "She works here."

"Pete said you two were on the dock yesterday."

"If you don't at least try to get to sleep, I'm leaving."

"I could fall asleep faster if you'd lie down next to me." She pouts in a way that's meant to be sexy but bugs the hell out of me. I still haven't followed up on Zach's comment that Pat was upset the night she went missing. The longer I spend here, the less chance I'll get to talk to Jamie tonight.

"One more word and I'm out of here."

She makes a face and rolls over on her side with her back to me. I check my watch. Jamie should be home by now. In fact, if I hang around here much longer, it's going to be too late to go knocking on his door. I didn't see his mom there the last time, but she must live there. If she's anything like Reesie, she's not going to take kindly to a strange guy showing up at her house at all hours.

My head is throbbing worse than ever. I look around the room, wondering where Tracy might keep painkillers. There's only one shelf between the beds. I tiptoe over for a closer look. She's got the usual chick paraphernalia — hair bands, make-up, Brazilian Bikini Wax Microwave Kit. Girls really are another species.

I pick up a sequined shower bag. It seems as likely a place as any to stash medication. Sure enough, birth-control pills are right on top. I push them aside and see something that gives me such a shock I drop the bag. It crashes to the floor, the contents scattering in all directions. Tracy flips over and vaults off the bed, pouncing on her belongings like a tigress protecting her cubs.

"What do you think you're doing, going through my stuff?" she shrieks.

"What are you doing with my sister's necklace?"

She glares at me. "Tricia gave it to me. What business is it of yours?"

"*I* gave it to her." My mind is so heavy with images that I sink down on Pat's bed and barely notice.

Me: *How could you give it away? Don't you remember when I bought it for you in that little seaside store in Atlantic City?*
Pat: *Of course I remember. We spent hours trolling the beach for sea creatures. I was so disappointed there weren't*

any, but all you did was nag me to put my sandals back on in case I stepped on a sea urchin. You could never just enjoy the moment; you were always obsessing on the next thing that might go wrong.

ME: *And you always acted like nothing ever could. You were only fourteen, but even then you were so sure of yourself.*

PAT: *When I saw that starfish pendant, I pleaded with Dad to buy it, but he'd blown all his cash on gas and roadside motels just to show me the ocean.*

ME: *So I spent every penny I'd saved from my paper route.*

PAT: *I still can't figure out how you managed it. How did you have enough money? You didn't steal it, did you?*

ME: *No. But thanks for the vote of confidence. I told the shop lady it was for you. She'd seen you admiring it. I think she wanted you to have it almost as much as I did. Anyway, she let me have it for the cash I had. I don't think I paid more than half what it should have been, but she was just like everyone else in the universe. She didn't want to disappoint you.*

PAT: *Are you sure that's the way it was, Luke? You were the one who got the great price. Maybe it was you she didn't want to disappoint.*

ME:

"She never took it off," I say accusingly, but I'm not sure whom I'm accusing. I know Pat changed when she came here, but that starfish meant something, at least to me. Even when she left for Utila and I wouldn't say good-bye to her, I snuck enough of a peek to make sure she was still wearing it. Could she really have cared so little about me that she'd just give it away?

"I'm sorry," Tracy says, tearing up. "I told you we were close. I don't know what to say. Do you want it back?"

"No."

I stand up and walk to the door. "I have to go now."

I don't wait for her reply as I slam out of the room.

It's a moonless night, dark and foreboding, the wind fierce and unforgiving. I can smell rain coming. I start walking and don't slow down till I'm on the outskirts of town. The cement road turns into a potholed dirt track; streetlights peter out and darkness closes in. The houses become fewer and most seem to be empty. No lights shine from their windows.

There are long stretches of vacant lots. The few scrubby palms are windswept, their frayed leaves whipping back and forth like the extended arms of frenzied celebrants summoning the dark forces. There must be a seawall running along the edge of the lots because the sea roils against it, sending up spray as the sheltered curve of the harbor flattens out to unprotected coast. Gone are the postcard blues and greens of the daytime; the water is obsidian black.

The police report said Pat drowned off McCrae's dock at the far eastern end of the island, the direction I'm walking. I wonder if it was a brooding night like this, the air saturated with unshed tears. Was she feeling the way I do now, angry and betrayed? Would that have been enough to make her go into a sea like this? She always felt most at home in the water. It comforted her in a visceral way, not unlike the way it terrifies me. If she was upset, it's entirely possible she'd want to be in the water, but maybe it wasn't comfort she sought. Could something have made her want to drown herself? That would be unthinkable for the sister I knew. But so would giving away my necklace.

"Dude, what are you doing way out here?"

I turn to see Zach huffing up the road after me.

"I shouted at you when you passed the Spiny Starfish, but you didn't even slow down." He stops walking and leans over, his hand on his side, panting. "Shit," he wheezes. "Gotta cut back on the smokes."

"Which dock is McCrae's?" I didn't realize until I asked that that's where I'm going. I'm not sure I want company, but one dock looks much like another out here. I won't find it alone.

"You're almost there," he says, straightening up.

"Show me," I say, and continue walking.

Zach trots to catch up. "Slow down, man, it's just past the next house."

I stop when I come to a laneway running between an empty lot and a boarded-up home. Looking around, I see that all the buildings out here are deserted. What kind of mind-set was Pat in to come all the way out here on her own? She could have been attacked and no one would have heard her screams. Back home she would have been way more sensible than that. Pat was a risk-taker when it served a purpose, but she wasn't foolhardy.

"Is this the way to the dock?" I start down the path with-out waiting for his answer. Zach is right behind me, so I guess I'm heading in the right direction.

The dock's in bad shape; several planks are missing and it's completely caved in at the end. Seawater smashes over one side, briefly submerging it with every wave. I'm hesitant to walk out on it. The opaque water gives me the creeps. I peer into it, searching for a telltale fin. Sharks hunt at night. Pat knew that as well as I do. I take a deep breath and step onto the dock. It writhes like a living thing beneath my feet. I have to force myself to hold my ground and not retreat to the safety of the shore. I feel Zach step onto the dock behind me.

"Do you know where they found her clothes?" I ask.

"Right at the end."

"How is that even possible?" I turn to him and see my own anxiety reflected in his eyes.

He shrugs.

I take a few more tentative steps, feeling the swell of the surf as it batters the dock. I think the boards will give way any minute. I look apprehensively at the water hammering against the planks. I'm sure it's not very deep this close to shore, but I have no desire to test that theory. The dock shudders and I shudder right along with it. For my sister to venture out on a dock like this, she'd have to have had a good reason. If they hadn't found her clothes piled at the end, I could believe she was swept into the sea by accident.

Is it my imagination or are the waves getting bigger?

"Storm's close," says Zach in reply to my unasked question.

I expect him to suggest we take cover, but instead he lurches past me, almost running, right to the point where the dock splinters and slopes into the sea. He drops to his knees and pukes over the edge.

"Treat for the fishes," he shouts, grinning sheepishly back at me.

"You been drinking, Zach?" I have to raise my own voice to be heard over the sound of the surf.

He nods and stays crouched over the water. It's not safe for him to be out there.

"Come back now," I shout.

Zach clings tightly to the planks as he shifts to a sitting position and swings his legs over the side, inches above the foaming ocean. A wave crashes over the end of the dock, soaking him. The dock sways.

"Zach! Get back here, now!"

"Can't." I can hardly hear his voice over the breakers. He rests his elbows on his knees, his head in his hands.

"I'm not kidding, Zach," My heart is pounding now, just like that other night. The intervening years dissolve into my fear and I'm nine years old again. "Get back here!" I bellow, as angry as I am scared.

A huge wave crashes against the dock, soaking him again.

And then the rain starts. It pelts down so thick and fast that I lose sight of Zach. My heart jumps right out of my chest when I think he's been swept out to sea. But a crack of lightning gives me a flash of him, hunched over his hands and knees, clinging limpet-like to the thrashing dock.

"ZACH!" I scream.

His answer is drowned out by another wave cresting over the dock like a tsunami. Against every instinct in my body, I sprint toward the wall of water and catch his shirt just as his legs slip out from under him. The dock tips us both seaward, but I scramble back, tugging him with me.

"We have to get off the dock," I cry, catching sight of another foamy white monster barreling toward us.

We scuttle on all fours (actually three for me, because I don't let go of him until we reach land). The rain is bucketing down. There are no trees this close to the shoreline, so we hop the fence of the abandoned house and dash underneath it. Maybe that's why most of the buildings in town are on stilts. We collapse on the cement foundation, shivering.

"Tropical storms come up fast," Zach says.

"Ya think?"

I lie flat on my back, listening to the rain pounding on the metal roof of the house, and I close my eyes.

ME: *It doesn't make sense, Pat. You're too smart to throw away your life. Why did you even come out here?*

PAT: *Are you sure you're asking the right question?*

ME:

"Cripes!" Zach's voice jolts me upright. "I almost forgot. Mini Mike gave me a message for you."

"Mini Mike?"

"Yeah, you know, Spiny Starfish Mike."

"The owner?" I recall the Goliath I served coffee. "I never got his name."

"It was something about the radio." Zach wrinkles his forehead.

"What about the radio?"

Zach puts his head between his knees.

"Was it about last night?" I suggest. "Dr. Jake said there was chatter about us on the radio."

"No." Zach says. "More important than that. About Tricia."

He starts taking raspy, deep breaths. "I think I'm going to puke again."

I count to ten in my head to stop myself from dragging him to his feet to give him a good shake. He leaps up and runs to the edge of the house, kneeling down and dry heaving over the grass.

"Sorry," he says, staggering back and plopping down beside me. "There was a distress call from the Shark Center the night Tricia went missing. No one knows whose voice it was, just some guy saying there'd been an accident and asking Dr. Dan to come quickly. He's the only doctor on the island."

"An accident? What kind of accident?"

"No one knows," he says. "When Dr. Dan got there, the place was completely deserted. He figured it was some kind of prank, so he never bothered mentioning it until tonight. Mike was asking everyone where they were the night Tricia went missing and it just came out."

We're both quiet for several minutes, trying to make sense of this new information.

"Did you know Tricia got on the wrong side of some drug dealers?" I ask.

Zach looks at me in surprise. "She did go a little ape-shit when this drug plane dumped its stash offshore. But I didn't know she actually did anything about it."

"She didn't invite you to any kind of anti-drug meeting?"

He shakes his head. "Seriously, man, that's not exactly my scene."

"Yeah, I'm with you there."

"So you think they had something to do with her disappearance?"

"Maybe. What do you know about drug planes refueling at the airport at night?"

"I dunno . . . there're always stories." He pauses to give it some thought. "I have an idea!" he exclaims. "We should do a stakeout, bring a few beers, sleep up in the woods behind the runway. If there are drug planes refueling, we could catch them in the act!"

I nod. "Worth a try. It still won't prove they did something to Pat, but maybe it would be enough to get the police to start looking for her again. But, first, I need to speak to Jamie about a fight he had with my sister. The way I see it, either the drug lords did something to her, which would go together with trying to scare her with voodoo dolls, or she had some kind of fight with Jamie and did something reckless to herself — though I'm not really buying that theory."

"Or a voodoo witch put a hex on her," Zach adds.

"Yeah, but I think we should consider that our least likely option."

"The main thing is, she's still alive, right?" Zach looks both hopeful and frightened at the same time. "Because she speaks to you, so she has to be alive."

"Absolutely," I say. I wish I felt as confident as I sound.

Zach smiles. "Okay." He gets unsteadily to his feet and walks to the edge of the house nearest the road. "So, are we gonna jet?"

"It's still pouring," I point out.

Zach lifts the edge of his shirt and twists it so water streams out. "You worried we might get wet?"

"Fair enough." I jump up and follow him out from under the house.

——

We run most of the way to Jamie's house, making only brief pit stops under trees to catch our breath. We slide and hit the pavement several times on sodden, rotting fruit, treacherous as ice, so we're scraped up pretty bad by the time we finally arrive. We keep up the pace straight up Jamie's path and hesitate only when we get to the steps. Neither of us wants to drip water on Reesie's veranda.

"Do you think we should shout from here?" Zach roars over the sound of the storm.

"No," I shout back, a little more forcefully than I intended. The thought of Reesie catching us outside her house at this time of night actually makes me sweat. "You don't happen to know which bedroom is Jamie's, do you?"

Zach walks around the side of the house, looking up at the darkened windows. I follow him around the back, where he stops, fixated on one window in particular.

"Have you been in his room before?" I ask.

"Once," he says.

"Is this it?"

"I think so. Yeah, I'm sure it is. Definitely."

He's already hunting for pebbles to throw at the window so I help, and before long we're both standing under Jamie's window with our hands full of shards of wet coral.

"You want to go first?" I ask.

"Cosmic."

Zach winds up. I have a moment of panic that he's going to chuck it so hard, he actually breaks the window, but his pitch goes wide and doesn't even hit the house. Considering there's at least eight feet of wall on either side of the window, I find that strangely impressive.

"Sports were never my thing," Zach sighs.

"I wouldn't say that, buddy. It takes real skill to miss that bad."

I toss my own pebble and hit the window dead on. Pat always said I'd be good at sports if I gave up the drugs. But I really only had time for the one hobby.

We wait, but there's no response. I pitch a couple more bits of coral. They all hit their mark, to no effect.

"Maybe he can't hear us over the rain," suggests Zach.

"Good point."

I look at the one fistful of ammo I have left and the one Zach's still holding.

"All together?" I suggest.

"Let's rock 'n' roll," he agrees.

We launch our missiles like there's no tomorrow, and also like there's no glass in the window, which there is. Unfortunately.

Who would have guessed you could shatter glass with a few bits of coral?

The window, what's left of it, flies open and Reesie's head pops out.

CHAPTER 12

I turn to glare at Zach, who has totally disappeared. It takes me a second to track him to where he's scurried under the house.

"Don't tell her I'm here," he hisses. Since he's now immediately under her and closer to her than me, he's wasting his breath.

"Get out from under my house, Zach O'Donell!" Reesie barks before she turns her ire on me.

I consider joining Zach. If we make a break for it, we could probably get past the gate before she catches us. But knowing her, she'd be on my doorstep before long, and even if we tried to wait her out at a bar, I'd have to go back to my room eventually.

"Good evening, Reesie." I smile innocently. "How are things?"

"You come to break my window, at midnight, in the middle of a thunderstorm, to ask me that?" she demands. "What're you smoking?"

I decide a different approach is in order.

"You're looking lovely tonight."

"Don't say that to her, man," groans Zach, surprisingly full of advice for a guy who's still hiding under a house.

"Oh, I see, you're thinking you're Romeo," she says, her eyes darker than the night. "You just wait here, Romeo. I need to go fetch something. Now where did I put that buckshot?"

She's going to kill me. I should've hidden when I had the chance.

"Reesie, who's that you be talkin' to?" An older woman appears at the window.

Reesie pauses and gives me a warning look before she answers. "It's just a friend, Mama."

"What your friend be doin' callin' at this time of night?" scolds Reesie's mom, barely glancing in my direction. "You know better than that, girl. What have I told you about boys? You gotta respect yourself if . . ."

"What's goin' on out there?" calls a third voice. A tiny wrinkled woman, with hair shooting straight up like a Muppet, nudges Reesie and her mother out of the way to give me the once-over.

"Who you be?" she demands.

"It's the brother of that girl, Nanny." Reesie's disembodied voice is barely audible.

"I told you not to call her *that girl*, Clarice Doreen," says the Muppet, not taking her beady eyes off me. "She be your brother's fiancée. Don't matter whether she be dead or alive. You pay her some respect.

"What you be doin' here this time of night, boy?" she goes on. "And why you be playin' around in the rain like a duck on Fish Friday? You a duck?"

"No, ma'am," I say. I don't add that if I were a duck, I would have winged it out of here long before now.

"Then you best get your soggy backside inside. Reesie, wake your brother. This boy's gonna need some dry clothes."

The Muppet disappears from the window, and I turn on Zach. "Don't even think of leaving me to do this on my own," I say.

Zach looks away guiltily but follows me around to the front of the house, where all three females are lined up on the porch. The older two show the corrosion of too many years in harsh sunlight and salt air, yet still have Reesie's same clear, steady eyes. Together Zach and I climb the steps, as slowly as can be done without actually walking backwards.

"You didn't tell me there be a second one." Reesie's mom gives her an accusing look.

"You remember Zach, Mama," says Reesie.

"He the boy who smokes marijuana and got no family?" demands the Muppet.

Reesie and her mom exchange glances.

"Nanny . . ." starts Reesie's mom.

"Don't understand how a mama's gonna throw out she own child," continues Nanny, warming to the subject. "It not be natural. Why even a she-dog gonna look after she —"

"Come inside, boys," interrupts Reesie's mom, holding the door open for us.

I put a hand on Zach's shoulder and give it a squeeze as we file through. I wish I'd let him escape when he had the chance.

We enter a small living room crowded with two tattered couches, several armchairs and a collection of wooden side tables that look straight out of some expensive interior design store, beautiful and totally out of place.

Jamie is just coming out of what I assume to be his bedroom, which I can't help but notice is on the opposite side of the house from where we were pitching coral.

"Hey," I say to Jamie.

"Hey," he answers. "You guys want to come in my room and get changed? I've got some towels in there already."

"You hurry on up," says Reesie's mom. "I'll fix you some tea. You boys must be half froze."

"Best fix 'em some food, too," chimes in Nanny. "That boy be an orphan, you know. Are they both orphans? I can't abide a woman who doesn't know how . . ."

We don't hear the rest of her rant as Jamie hustles us into his room and shuts the door. His room is as small as mine at the Shark Center, but the matching single beds and chest of drawers are definitely a big step up. Obviously handmade, like the tables in the other room, they use the same contrast of light and dark wood to highlight the sweeping lines of the curved head- and footboards. A small boy is sitting on one of the beds, staring at us intently as we crowd into the narrow space between the beds and take the towels Jamie hands us.

"Is this him?" asks the boy, gawking at us as we strip off.

"This is my brother, Donny," says Jamie, squeezed into the corner between his bed and the chest.

"Are you Reesie's boyfriend?" Donny asks.

I catch Jamie making some kind of a slashing motion out of the corner of my eye, but he fakes a stretch when I turn to look at him directly.

I turn back to Donny and blink.

"She's available, if you're interested," continues Donny.

"We best be getting out there," Jamie says, though Zach is still in his undershorts and I don't have a shirt on yet.

"She talks about you all the time," says Donny.

"He exaggerates," says Jamie, making big eyes at his brother.

I yank on the shirt and head for the door.

"Do not," insists Donny indignantly. "She said Trish's brother was a nice boy!"

"Do you need help getting that shirt on, Zach?" I ask, my hand on the knob. I'll leave him behind if I have to.

"I could put in a good word for you," offers Donny, as I open the door. Zach and Jamie follow me out, Zach still pulling on his shirt.

Reesie's mom leads the way into a tidy, compact kitchen with polished pine counters that match built-in cabinets and possibly the most beautiful dining set I've ever seen. The table and each chair are all different, their edges following the natural contours of the tree they were hewn from, rather than being straight-cut and angular. Reesie's mom directs us to sit, while Reesie puts steaming cups of tea in front of us and Nanny lays out buns and jam.

"That be my homemade coconut bread," she says proudly, "and my mango preserves."

"Best bread on the island," says Reesie.

"Best bread in all the Bay Islands," her grandmother corrects.

"All of Honduras," her mother adds.

"The entire planet," Reesie says, grinning.

"The universe," Jamie chimes in and they all laugh. It's obviously a familiar routine.

I suddenly get a pang of something like nostalgia, which is stupid because I've never eaten homemade bread with homemade jam at a handmade kitchen table. And I've definitely never experienced a family with little education and even less money who don't think they need a bottle to ease the shame of that.

I look over at Zach, thinking how much worse it must be for him. At least I have a family. What does he have?

But I discover, to my surprise, that what he has is a big dopey grin on his face as he polishes off two buns in the time it's taken me to butter my first. His undiluted happiness to be part of this family, if only for a short time, takes the edge off my own gloomy thoughts. I chow down on the food, and when I tell Nanny it really is the best bread I've ever tasted, I'm not exaggerating.

After serving us, Reesie and her mom set out tea and plates for everyone, and the whole gang of them sit down with Zach and me. I also didn't grow up in a family who sat down to meals together, so this feels weird, yet natural at the same time. I wonder how different my life would be if my parents had taken the time to sit across the dinner table from me once a day. It's not that it never happened, but it was an event usually reserved for holidays and birthdays.

"So what be your business here at this time of night?" asks Nanny.

I shift uncomfortably. I hadn't expected to interview Jamie in front of his entire clan.

"We're investigating Tricia's disappearance," Zach pipes up.

I slather jam on my coconut bread bun with the undivided focus of a military operation. I don't have to look up to feel everyone's eyes on me.

"Jamie, where were you on the night she disappeared?" Zach continues.

I take a giant bite and a clump of fruit-filled jam slides off and hits the front of my shirt. I hunch forward, hoping no one noticed, and a large chunk of mango dislodges itself and lands on the beautifully polished table. Pretending to pull my plate closer, I cover the mess and look up to find the entire group of them, even Zach, staring at me.

"You be thinkin' that's a magic plate?" asks Nanny. "Isn't no magic plate gonna make that mess disappear. It's still right there under your plate. Go on and look."

"Sorry," I mumble, sweat beading on my forehead.

"Isn't no nevermind," says Nanny, chortling. "You're a nervous sort, aren't ya? Not at all like your sister."

I sit up straighter.

"You knew my sister?"

"Course," says Reesie's mom, in surprise. "She was around here most every day."

"What?" say Reesie and I in unison.

"Trish was always happy when we spent time here," says Jamie, his eyes misting over. "Sometimes I felt like she loved my family as much as she loved me."

"You never told me she was around all the time," snaps Reesie. "I still don't understand why you all thought you had to keep that from me?"

"We told her to come when you were at work," says Nanny. "That be my idea."

Nanny leans over to me and confides, "Since her dad died, Reesie throws cold water on every relationship the poor boy tries to have. She doesn't want to lose him too, ya see."

"That's not true." Reesie scowls.

"Is so," says Nanny, "and it's nothin' to be ashamed of. Natural you look out for ya brother. But Trish was a good girl. You would have took to her in time."

"I liked her already," Reesie grouses. "If anyone had cared to ask me, I would have told you that!"

"I wanted to tell you about her," says Jamie. "But Trish said not to hurry. She didn't want you to feel like she was crowding you out. She wanted to make friends with you first. She was so excited when I told her how much you appreciated that book she gave you. She was always talking about how smart you were and how we needed to convince you to go back to school."

"We were all sorry to lose her," Reesie's mom says, reaching across the table to squeeze Jamie's arm as she looks at me.

I meet her eyes. They're so full of sympathy, I find myself fighting back tears. I remind myself that just because they believe Pat's gone doesn't make it true. When I shift my focus away from Reesie's mom so I don't start bawling, I notice an embroidered wall hanging behind her entreating God to bless this home. The neat cross-stitching reminds me of something, but it takes a minute before I put it together. It's the same stitching as on the voodoo dolls. I'm sure of it.

"I be teachin' her my secret recipe for coconut bread," says Nanny, breaking into my thoughts.

"You did not!" gasps Reesie.

I turn back to three generations of women looking at each other, and I can almost hear the words flying between them.

Reesie sighs. "An island woman doesn't give up her recipe for coconut bread to anyone except her own daughters," she explains.

"Sometimes not even to them, if they don't deserve it," says Nanny, scowling at Reesie's mom.

"I never had much patience in the kitchen," Reesie's mom explains. "Reesie used to help Nanny with the bread till she got work cleanin' the dive hotels. Then Nanny did it alone till your sister came along."

"She had the gift," Nanny says. "All it takes is a gentle hand and a patient spirit."

Gentle and patient — two adjectives I would never use to describe my sister. No question she was good at everything she set her mind to, and she certainly made her share of meals for us when Mom was too depressed or drunk to bother. But we were lucky if she took time to cut a few vegetables; more often, it was canned soup and crackers.

I rest my head on my hand and close my eyes, calling up memories of Pat, trying to picture her in this kitchen, her long black hair in a loose knot at the nape of her neck, her green eyes, usually so sharp, softened by the soothing repetition of kneading dough.

Suddenly this gentle image morphs into another, and the nightmare floods my consciousness: shredded clothing, tangled hair, one eye blankly staring, the other a cavernous hole. My sister's body, battered. If this image has any truth, someone did this to her.

CHAPTER 13

"What were you and Pat fighting about the night she disappeared?" I demand, pinning Jamie with suspicious eyes.

The temperature in the room drops several degrees as he returns my gaze, his brow creased. I feel Reesie staring at me. No telling what Nanny and Reesie's mom are thinking as we wait for Jamie's answer.

"She wanted to stay on here permanently," he says finally, as if he's carried the words inside him for a long time and laying down the burden of them is both a release and a betrayal. "But I told her to go home."

"Why'd you go and do that for?" asks Nanny, while I'm still processing the idea that Pat never intended to come home.

"I wanted her to finish her education. An education isn't something to be passed up lightly." He's looking at Reesie when he says this. She looks right back at him, her chin jutting out.

"I promised to wait for her but she wouldn't believe me. She thought I'd get fed up waiting and find another girl."

"I knew she was a smart one," says Reesie. It's not clear if she's referring to Pat's decision to give up school or her distrust of Jamie, but he rounds on her angrily.

"You never should have quit. I could have supported all of us. I darn well wasn't going to let her make the same mistake." His voice shakes with emotion. "I would have waited a lifetime for her. But she went ahead and got Dr. Jake to keep her on. Told me she'd decided, like I didn't have any say in the matter."

Every word is a piercing dart. I feel weak as the implication of what he's saying seeps in like poison. She was leaving me to my drugs and my apathy. She was leaving me with a mother too hungover to show up for breakfast most mornings and a dad consumed by the guilt of that. This wasn't just a summer job. She never intended to come back.

"She said she didn't want any other life but what she had here," continues Jamie, unable to shut his damn mouth now that he's opened it. "She said this was her home now."

"Shut up!" I scream, not realizing I'm on my feet till Zach pushes back his chair and stands up too. "You're a goddamn liar! She wouldn't desert me for you. Is that what you expect me to believe? Did you kill her? Is that it? You tried to scare her with your voodoo, and then you murdered her because she still wanted to leave you."

Zach comes round the table to stand next to me. I think he's going to help me punch Jamie out, but instead he puts an arm around me and pulls me into a tight hug.

"Let go." I struggle against his chest, but he's surprisingly strong for such a wiry guy and he's holding on like his life depends on it, or maybe mine does.

The first sob tears at my insides like shards of glass. I bury my head in Zach's shoulder to hide the humiliation, but he takes it as some sort of sign and just hugs harder. I feel another arm on my back and then another, and I'm monkey in the middle of some insane group hug, which, like family dinners, is yet another thing we don't do at home.

"Let it out, child," says Reesie's mom. "There be no shame in grief."

"I need air," I gasp.

"Of course we care," croons Reesie's mom, her voice muffled in the crush of bodies.

"I think he said 'air'," says Reesie, who sounds farther away.

"You need to get your hearin' checked," chides Nanny. "Why would he say 'air'?"

"Because it's a hundred degrees in here and you all are suffocating him."

"Oh, dear," says Reesie's mom, and the tangle of bodies abruptly parts.

Light-headed, I lean over, putting my hands on my knees.

"You okay?" asks Zach.

I nod but don't rise until the dizziness subsides. Zach takes my arm and nudges me back to my chair.

"Reesie, warm up his tea," Nanny commands.

Reesie leans over and pours some fresh tea into my cup. For a split second, our eyes meet. She's biting her lip, but I can see the smile tugging at the corner. Suddenly I feel light-headed again, and it has nothing to do with oxygen deprivation. I can't help but wish that someday I might get a chance to explore this because I've never had this feeling about a girl before.

"Now what's this about voodoo?" she asks, taking her seat.

I flush, remembering my tirade. It suddenly seems highly unlikely that Jamie had anything to do with Pat's disappearance. I know I have to ask about the dolls, though. Their wall hanging is the first evidence I've found of someone knowing how to do a cross-stitch, though I suspect it's not a rare skill around here.

I pull out the voodoo doll I took from under Tracy's step. My own is still drying out in my room.

"I found this voodoo doll back at the Shark Center. There was a similar one under my step two days ago, and Tracy said there was one under Pat's porch the day before she disappeared."

"And you think I put it there?" asks Jamie incredulously.

"Well," I say slowly, realizing how stupid it sounds. "Tracy thought you, or maybe Reesie, might be practicing voodoo."

"Voodoo?" says Reesie, the warmth of moments before gone from her eyes. "Why would she be thinking we're doing voodoo? Has she ever seen me slicing off chicken heads or dancing around in a trance?"

"No."

"Then maybe she's seen me hiding those dolls. Is that it?"

"I don't think so."

"Well, she must have seen something. Maybe she saw me chanting or hexing people."

"No, I think she would have mentioned that."

"So she didn't see me or my brother doing anything voodoo-like, but she thinks we're the ones planting the dolls. Is that it?"

"Yeah," I admit, knowing I'm not going to like what's coming next.

"And you believed her?" Her voice is shaking. I can't tell if she's hurt or angry. I have a feeling it's a bit of both, and that makes me feel worse than anything.

"No, not really."

"But you asked Jamie if he was doing voodoo on your sister."

"It was just an idea." I can feel the sweat popping out on my forehead again.

"Tell me, Luke, do you think everyone on Utila is practicing voodoo?"

I knew this was coming.

"Leave the boy alone, Clarice Doreen," says her mom. "Can't you see you be embarrassin' him?"

"Well, I sure hope so." Reesie crosses her arms over her chest, but a look from her mom ends the interrogation.

I want to apologize but that seems like admitting guilt, and I never even believed in the voodoo crap, at least not much. I get to my feet.

"I think we've taken enough of your time tonight," I say politely. "Thanks for the tea and dry clothes."

"You be welcome here anytime," says Reesie's mom firmly. "My name's Miss Hettie. You get yourself into any trouble, you tell someone to call Miss Hettie. I mean that. And don't let Reesie be scarin' you. She be all bark."

"Ya come back for some more of my coconut bread," adds Nanny.

Jamie walks us to the door. I'm surprised to see Reesie trailing behind. The two of them follow Zach and me out to the porch.

As we reach the steps, Jamie puts a light hand on my arm.

"Luke," he begins, his voice hoarse with emotion. "I've had a lot of time to think about what Trish might have been feeling the night she went missing." He meets my eyes with a bleak look. "The fact is, her death is on me. She thought I was rejecting her. I know that. I went back later that night to tell her how sorry I was. It was such a stupid fight. Of course I wanted her to stay on, every bit as much as she wanted to stay. I just didn't want her giving up everything to be with me. I know there's nothing I can ever do to make it up to you and your family, but you have to know how sorry I am." Jamie offers his hand and I take it, again noticing the firm, rough feel of it and the warmth.

"I do," I say, and I mean it. I don't think their fight caused my sister to drown herself, though. What Jamie doesn't understand is that Pat and I grew up in a family where screaming matches were a daily occurrence. There's no way a simple disagreement would push Pat over the edge. In fact, hearing about her plans and meeting this family only makes me more certain she would have fought hard to hang on to the life she was building here, which means someone else is responsible for her disappearance.

"Hey, do you know if my sister was mixed up in the drug runners that have been refueling at the airport at night?"

Jamie drops my hand and steps back.

"Drug runners?" He and Reesie exchange glances.

"Where'd you get a notion like that?" Reesie asks carefully.

"I ran into a guy who said Tricia might have been trying to make trouble for the drug runners."

A faraway look crosses Jamie's face. He seems so sad, I regret bringing it up.

"I told your sister to stay away from those people, but when she's got a bee in her bonnet, not hell or high water could dislodge it."

I nod sympathetically. "So do you think she could have done something to make them come after her?"

"You know, it never occurred to me. The plane that went down had Red Cross insignia on it, but that was just a cover-up. They found a Venezuelan flag underneath. The landings had been going on for months before the crash. Trish was already riled up, but when they dropped those drugs in the water, I'd never seen her so mad. She said she was going to go up there one night and confront them. I made her promise me she wouldn't, but the night she disappeared . . . I was so sure she was upset about our fight. But now that you mention it —"

"Jamie," interrupts Reesie. "It's late. We should all be getting to bed. I'm sure we'll all be thinking more clearly in the morning."

I scowl at her. "Finish what you were saying, Jamie."

"I did hear a plane that night, but that doesn't mean it had anything to do with Trish. You let me look into it, Luke. These are dangerous people. There's not much I can do for Trish anymore except keep her brother safe. Promise me you'll leave this to me."

"People are best minding their own business," Reesie announces. I'm not sure which one of us she's bossing around.

"You make all of the furniture in there?" I ask, deliberately changing the subject.

"Yeah."

"You could make a bundle back home producing work like that."

He gives a hint of a smile. "You're not so different from your sister after all; she was always saying that. But what would I be doing chasing money a thousand miles away when there's everything a person needs to be happy right here?"

I think about that for a minute. "I guess you must have won that argument."

"Trish is gone." Jamie's grief is suddenly so palpable, I wonder how I could have ever doubted him. "I didn't win anything."

I start down the steps but look back when he continues.

"One thing you need to know, Luke. She didn't choose me instead of you. She talked about you all the time, even talked about bringing you down here."

I nod.

ME: *You weren't planning to come back, were you?*

PAT: *If you had the chance to be part of this family, wouldn't you leave ours in a heartbeat?*

ME: *It doesn't work like that, Pat. You don't get to choose. You make the best of the family you've got and love them the best way you know how.*

PAT: *Is that what Mom was doing when she tried to kill herself? Or what you were doing every time you shut me out with your drugs and booze?*

ME:

"I'm sure you're right," I say to Jamie.

"You're welcome here anytime, Luke. I hope you know that."

"Sure." I'm striding toward the gate, my chest tight with everything I'm struggling not to feel — hurt, betrayal, anger, guilt. Even when I find my sister, this is something I'll never change my opinion about. She gave up on us, all of us.

I hear the door shut behind us. I think they've both gone back inside so I'm surprised to hear Reesie's voice as we reach the gate. "You're planning on going up there, aren't you?"

I stop and turn. Zach, close on my heels, stops too.

"I don't know what you're talking about."

"She's talking about us investigating the drug dealers," Zach hisses.

I sigh.

Reesie moves forward into the porch light, her hands on her hips. "You heard what Jamie said."

"Who died and made him ruler of the planet?" says Zach, stepping behind me, so she doesn't have a clear view of him.

"You know she can tell it's you who's talking, right?"

"Shh," he whispers. "She'll hear you."

"So you and the brainchild are gonna go investigating drug runners?"

"We haven't made any decisions about going up there," I lie.

"You boys don't have the first clue about investigating," she says. "Have you even been to the police yet to ask them what happened?"

"We were going to do that tomorrow," Zach blusters.

"Good," says Reesie. "Then I'll meet you out front of the Shark Center at twelve tomorrow. Don't be late."

"Show-off," says Zach loudly — after Reesie's gone inside.

"Good comeback, buddy." I pretend I didn't notice he'd waited till she was out of hearing range. We high-five and Zach smiles happily, before a frown crosses his face.

"We *are* going up to the airport tonight, right?"

"You bet."

CHAPTER 14

It's around two in the morning by the time we're squatting in some spindly bushes near the edge of the runway. Though the rain has stopped, the ground is squelchy underfoot and we're both in flip-flops. I have only a vague notion of how this is going to go down.

First we need to confirm that there really are drug planes using the Utila runway on a regular basis. Then we have to find out if they had anything to do with my sister's disappearance. I don't know how I'm going to find that out, short of asking them directly. The drug runners clearly saw her as a threat. But if they did something to Pat, they're not going to admit it. Our best option is probably to find out if there is drug running going on and then get the police involved. Getting jumped by Bobby's guys proves that they had it in for her.

Just as I'm reaching this conclusion, there's the unmistakable drone of a plane circling overhead. My heart starts thumping. The plane does a full circle above and is starting a second when a brilliant spotlight flips on, illuminating the runway. And us.

I hit the dirt, or more accurately mud, while Zach stands up and shades his eyes, peering into the light.

"Zach, get down!" I hiss.

"I'm trying to see who turned on the light."

"They'll see you. Get down!"

Zach drops to his knees, but we both realize it's too late when we hear feet pounding the pavement, coming toward us. We can see the silhouettes of at least five guys, all carrying what look like automatic rifles. Despite my desire to interrogate them about my sister, running is the only sensible response.

"Run!" I shout.

I jump up and take off at top speed, crashing through bushes, covering more than a dozen yards in the other direction before I hit the sanctuary of the tree line. Only then do I realize Zach's not behind me. I wildly look around for him, until I realize in horror what he's done. He's taken my instruction to run, but gone straight at the gunmen. Now he's struggling with two guys, while two more point rifles at him and another raises his gun preparing to bring it crashing down on Zach's head. In the chaos, everyone has forgotten the plane, which has already started its descent and is heading directly for them.

I'm frozen in indecision at the horror of Zach's immediate danger and the shock of a plane about to plow into him. I race back toward Zach. Maybe I can hurl myself at him and knock him out of the hands of the drug runners and the path of the plane at the same time. But seconds after touching down on the tarmac, the pilot must have spotted the people on the ground because the plane veers sharply to one side, careening off the runway. The drug runners drop Zach and turn to watch their own plane hurtling into the bushes. My heart explodes against my ribcage as I realize it's now heading straight for me. I swerve just in time, only to be knocked over by the force of the wind it stirs up as it barrels past. A screeching clatter signals a wing being sheared off by a nearby tree. Finally, the plane lurches to a stop.

There's utter silence for the next few seconds. Zach and his attackers stare at the wreckage and I slither on my belly toward the runway, trying to get close enough to signal Zach. I'm dimly aware of a quiet dripping and the strong smell of gasoline. I don't realize the implications until I hear a *whoosh* and feel the heat of flames. I look back to see the plane ablaze and shudder to think of the pilot trapped inside. My attention is drawn back to the drug runners, as gunfire rings out from the darkness behind them. They hear it, too, and are thrown into panic, shouting as they race toward their burning plane. I have no choice — I have to run into the line of fire to save Zach. I scramble to my feet and am immediately thrown to the ground again by a deafening explosion, followed by snow falling everywhere.

The snow seems to confuse the drug runners as they halt in their tracks and put out their hands like they're trying to catch it. Zach does the same thing. Only when he licks his hand do I realize what it is.

"Zach, get out of there!" I scream.

Another shot rings out and the bad guys resume their sprint for the forest, completely ignoring Zach and me. The sound of an engine draws my attention to the far end of the runway, where a truck is just emerging into the light. Armed men in military fatigues clamber off the back. All at once, a second beam of light shines down from above. Looking up, I track the source to a helicopter hovering just overhead.

"Put your hands behind your heads and lie down on the ground!" a voice booms.

More gunfire rings out. I hit the dirt and am relieved to see Zach doing the same. "We should have run while we could," I mutter.

"Are they going to arrest us?" Zach is on the ground next to me. We can barely hear each other over the chaos of shouting, chopper wings and pounding feet.

"No. We didn't do anything wrong. But let me do the talking."

Zach nods. I don't know how I'm going to get us released if we do get arrested. Neither of us has enough cash for a lawyer. Would Dr. Jake bail me out? He's going to regret ever offering to help me.

Three heavily armed guys are bearing down on us from the copter, and a dozen or so men are making their way over from the truck. Every one of them has a weapon trained on us.

"On your knees," orders one of the copter guys. He's close enough now that I can read the logo on his shirt: DEA. I'm not sure if I'm reassured or scared that he's a fellow American.

"You don't understand —" I start but he cuts me off.

"Do you boys realize you've just destroyed weeks of surveillance? Do you have any idea what the consequences are for impeding an ongoing investigation? If it was up to me, we'd have let the traffickers have you. Did I see one of you actually licking this stuff?"

Zach stares at the ground while I look around at the circle of furious faces.

"S-sorry," I stammer, not sure what to respond to first. "My sister, Pat —"

"I know all about your sister," he snaps. "We've had a dozen e-mails from her since she picked up on the drug trade passing through here. She even called a few times after we forced down the plane that dumped its cargo in the ocean. Your sister was pretty worked up about that. It wasn't our fault, of course, but your sister wouldn't let us hear the end of it."

"But how do you know who *I* am?"

The DEA guy nods to the guys who came in on the truck, local police by the looks of them. I follow his gaze and my jaw drops as Reesie steps out from behind the throng.

"I knew you were planning to come up here, so after you left me, I went straight to the police. It took some convincing to get them to call reinforcements, but it was that or spend the night listening to my nattering."

"I'm surprised they took so long," I say.

Reesie gives me a small smile, but Zach frowns. "We could have escaped on our own."

"So did the drug lords have something to do with Pat's disappearance?" I turn back to the DEA guy.

"We don't believe so. All I can tell you for certain is, she wasn't kidnapped and taken off the island. We've been monitoring them too closely for that. But I have to say there were a lot of people who would have liked to shut your sister up. Someone on the island could have done something to her."

"Didn't you investigate?"

"This is a foreign country, son. Our operations here are limited to monitoring the drugs making their way onto U.S. soil. If we had some proof your sister's death was drug-related, we could request an investigation, but all the reports we've had so far make suicide more likely."

"You can't believe my sister committed suicide!"

"No." He shakes his head. "Personally, I don't. I'm just telling you that unless we have evidence her disappearance is directly related to our work here, there's nothing we can do."

I hang my head in disappointment. I know I should be grateful Pat wasn't kidnapped by drug traffickers, despite her best efforts to antagonize them, but all it feels like is another dead end and more reckless behavior I can't make sense of.

"You kids need to go home now," says the DEA guy, gently but firmly.

I look up to find both Zach and Reesie watching me. Reesie steps forward and takes my arm. Zach grabs the other one, more forcefully than necessary, and with me awkwardly sandwiched between them, we lumber off the airstrip. The local military have mostly dispersed into the bush to look for the druggie ground crew, and the DEA guys are heading over to the remains of the plane. I hope I haven't really messed up their investigation. I'd like to think some good came from my sister's relentless pushiness.

"I don't get it," I say to no one in particular as we turn onto the road heading back to town.

"What's that, Luke?" Zach asks.

"Before she came here, Pat was vegan, clean living, hard-working, ambitious. She put my mom to bed when she'd had too much to drink. Made sure we always had some kind of dinner on the table, nagged me about my homework, even got me to bed on time before I was old enough to stand up to her. She was always doing the right thing and pushing everyone else to do right as well, me especially. So I understand why she'd take on drug dealers, particularly if they were endangering the reef. But I don't get the other stuff. Pete and Tracy said she was slutty, and Zach, you said she drank, and Mini Mike said she was eating meat. And, on top of it all, she was planning to give up her education, everything she'd been working toward her whole life. So why would she let go of some of her standards but hang on to the one that could get her killed?"

"Maybe because she could," says Reesie.

I give her a questioning look.

"From what you've said, your sister took on a lot of responsibility in your family. Maybe because your mom wasn't looking after you properly, your sister felt like she had to set a good example. It sounds like she was tryin' real hard to be perfect. But here no one was gonna get hurt if she let go a bit. She only had herself to be responsible for. I've told you before, tourist kids go a little crazy down here."

I nod, trying to fit this idea into everything else I never understood about Pat. "Then why is it that the only thing she didn't change was being a pushy, meddling, know-it-all?" I demand angrily. "Wouldn't you think if she were going for a total personality transplant, she could have dispensed with the one quality most likely to get her killed?"

Zach and Reesie are silent for several minutes.

"She didn't drink that much," says Zach finally.

"And I don't think my brother would have been planning to marry a girl with loose morals," Reesie adds. "Maybe the change wasn't as big as you think it was. Maybe she just loosened the jib a bit, let the sails out."

"I didn't want her to come down here," I confess, glad for the cover of darkness so I can't see Reesie's face. "But I knew she had to get away. Pat and I aren't like the usual kids you see here who've never had anything bad happen to them. I know you've both had your troubles, but I think most kids can jump into the ocean and really believe nothing's going to go wrong. I envy them their naive optimism. I wish I was that way. But the weird thing is, Pat wasn't naive. She knew as well as I did that the worst-case scenario was the one most likely to happen. Yet no matter how many times our lives came dangerously close to going off the rails, she never faltered. She lived her life in defiance of our reality. I loved that about her. I hated it, too.

"Then some stuff happened with my mom, and for the first time, I could see Pat losing her nerve. It's not that she didn't believe in herself anymore, but she didn't believe in us, or maybe just me. She didn't think we could survive without her. She started talking about deferring her scholarship and maybe taking a year off."

"So how'd she end up here?" asks Reesie.

I hesitate. I want to tell her the whole truth, but I'm really starting to like this girl. I don't want to disappoint her. I'm sick of disappointing people. "She got offered the internship," I say simply. "It was too good to pass up." I stop and we walk for several minutes in silence. Once again I've taken the coward's way out and left my sister holding the bag.

"She tried to talk it over with me before she accepted, but I didn't let her."

"How'd she feel about that?" asks Reesie, and I can hear the smile in her voice.

"She was pissed. I didn't even say good-bye."

"That must have made it easier for her to leave."

"She never looked back." My voice is tight, the memory still painful.

"There's some who see a problem and walk right on by. But others are always gonna look for a way to fix it."

"I know. That was my sister all over. I was her project for a lot of years. I guess it's not so surprising she found something else to get worked up about when she came down here."

"It's not surprising," Reesie agrees. "But I wasn't talking about your sister."

I stop walking and turn to her. Zach drops my arm and, for a moment, it's like Reesie and I are the only ones here. The clouds have cleared. Her face glimmers in the moonlight.

"What do you mean?"

"Your sister never could have left if she thought you still needed her. You made sure she knew you didn't want anything from her anymore."

"Then it's my fault she came down here?" I find it ironic that even when I don't tell Reesie the whole truth, she arrives at the same conclusion.

"You did the right thing, Luke. You had to let her go. Something tells me you spend a lot of time trying to make things right for other people."

"Ha! You really don't know me. I hurt everyone around me."

"Really? The only one I've seen you hurting is yourself."

"Whoa," exclaims Zach, making us both jump. "This is like 'Dr. Phil,' where people have all these secrets and stuff gets revealed, like affairs and children no one knew about, and Dr. Phil has to tell everyone what's really going on in their own lives because they don't even know until he tells them. It's really deep, like magma-deep. You should be a doctor, Reesie. You could go on TV and everything."

Reesie rolls her eyes, smiling. "We best be getting home," she says. We continue down the road, turning into her street without even discussing whether we're walking her home.

"Do you ever think about going back to school?" I ask tentatively. I remember the last time I asked her about school, it didn't go down too well, but we're almost at her gate so if she goes ballistic this time, I won't feel badly about leaving her to go the rest of the way herself.

"All the time," she admits. "But Jamie's already working as hard as any man can and, sooner or later, he's gonna want a wife and family. Whatever Mama and Nanny think, I want him to have his own life. He can't be supporting all of us forever."

"So I'm not the only one who spends too much time trying to engineer other people's happiness."

Her hand brushes my own and I think it's deliberate. I wish we were alone. We walk in silence for the next few yards till we're in front of her house.

"We still on for going to the police station tomorrow?" I ask, facing her as she leans on her gate. In fact, it's already tomorrow, I think guiltily. She's got to be at work in a couple of hours. Of course that's true of Zach, too, rocking on his heels behind me, eager to get going.

"Twelve sharp," confirms Reesie. "Outside the Shark Center."

"Twelve sharp," I repeat.

"Outside the Shark Center," Reesie repeats.

"We go to the police station," Zach adds.

Reesie and I both look at him and back at each other. I love the way her eyes look right at me, like she's seeing all of me. I want to be that guy I see reflected in her eyes because anything less wouldn't come close to being worthy of her. My eyes travel to her mouth, her lips curved in a tiny smile. I want to kiss her so badly, I find myself leaning forward and almost lose my balance. This girl unbalances me. But how do I kiss her? She's not like any girl I've ever been with. She's not drunk or stoned, for one thing, and she's not just out for a good time. To kiss her would mean something. I'd want it to mean something. But I don't know how to kiss a girl like that.

"So, we'll see you tomorrow then," I say, wanting to prolong the departure.

"Cosmic," adds Zach, grabbing the back of my shirt and giving it an insistent tug.

I exhale in frustration and start to turn away when Reesie suddenly cranes up and grazes my mouth with her lips. It happens so fast, I could almost believe I imagined it, and she's disappeared through her gate and into her house before I have time to react. I put my hand to my lips and imagine I can still feel her warmth, which I know is totally lame.

"Did you see that?" Zach squeaks. "Reesie just kissed you! That's like nuclear. What are we going to do?"

"I don't know," I say, watching her house, hoping she's peeking out from one of her darkened windows. I give a small wave.

"Okay," he says, struggling to sound calm, but his voice is still several octaves higher than normal. "I'm sure there's a way out of this. We'll talk to Jamie. No, wait, that's a bad idea. Reesie's his sister, he'll kill you. Maybe we could disappear for a while, until things cool down . . . but then how are we going to search for Tricia? Oh, man, this is so bad. It's like when Catwoman flirts with Batman and you know she's just toying with him, only this is so much worse because I think she's serious and Reesie is way, way scarier than Catwoman."

"Maybe I'll just have to go along with her for a while," I suggest, biting my lip to stop the happiness that's blossomed somewhere in the vicinity of my heart from taking over my whole face.

"Yeah," he agrees. "It's risky, but if you think you can pull it off, just till we come up with a way to let her down easy . . ."

"Just till then," I say, and I feel a ray of hope amid the darkness of my sister's disappearance.

CHAPTER 15

When Zach bursts into my room at the Shark Center a scant six hours later, I'm passed out on my bed still in my clothes.

"Dude, get in the shower," he orders. "Reesie's going to be here any minute. Unless you want her to see you all puffy-eyed and grubby like that." He pauses to consider this. "Nah." He shakes his head decisively. "That won't work. To a girl like Reesie, it would just be more proof that you need her."

He follows me into the shower room, completely fixated on how we're going to handle the "Reesie situation." It crosses my mind to tell him that if he'd just give me a few minutes alone with her, I've already figured out how I want to handle it, but something tells me Zach's not ready to hear that his new best friend is hot for a girl who terrifies him.

He talks non-stop about ways I can dump her as I let the water cascade over me. I don't hear most of what he's saying as I'm preoccupied with wondering if I'll get to kiss her again, though technically I didn't actually kiss her the first time. But if I get a second chance, I'm definitely going to be ready. The question is, how do I get a second chance with Zach bird-dogging my every move?

Back in my room, Zach plumps down on the extra bed while I pull on some clothes and inspect my T-shirt — clean, but after drying on the desk, so rumpled I might as well have slept in it.

I've never given much thought to being tidy before. I'm not a pig. I shower and everything, but I've never touched an iron in my life and I'm pretty sure my parents haven't either, so scruffy's always been my look. But I have a feeling Reesie's not the kind of girl who goes for scruffy.

"What do you think?" he demands.

"What?" I have no idea what he's talking about.

"The plan," he prompts.

I gawk at him. Still not a clue.

"To get rid of her," he prompts again.

"Oh, right. Sounds great."

"We'll need to be strong and stick together," he says.

"Okay." I wonder how I'm going to break it to him that I don't want to get rid of Reesie. We both jump at a rap on the door. Zach gives me a conspiratorial nod before he opens it.

"I've been waiting out front for ten minutes. What have you boys been doing in here?" Reesie stomps in, shouldering Zach out of the way.

"Working on strategy," I say, which is sort of true.

"Well, your first strategy should be to get your lazy butts to the meeting place on time since we already agreed we're going to the police station."

"We're coming now." I guess this probably isn't the best

moment to swoop in for a kiss, but seeing her again makes it really hard to put the idea out of my mind.

"We can't let her take over our investigation," Zach hisses as we fall into step behind Reesie, who strides down the path out of the Shark Center.

The sun's high in the sky and the heat is intense as we enter the narrow main street and walk single file, dodging pedestrians and the usual vehicles, mostly ATVs. When we turn off onto a side road going up the hill, huge trees on either side provide welcome, if steamy, shade. We spread out across the uneven cement track. It's just wide enough for a single car, though there's not much traffic beyond the occasional motorcycle. We walk in companionable silence. I catch Reesie's eye and she smiles. I smile back, even though I'm starting to feel anxious about what the police are going to say about my sister. Whatever they say, I know it will be bogus, just like the report they gave my parents. I'm just not sure I'm ready to hear it firsthand. Something of what I'm feeling must be visible on my face because Reesie swerves in and catches my hand and doesn't let go. I curl my fingers through hers and feel a little better, even though I catch an anxious look from Zach out of the corner of my eye.

"I didn't tell Jamie about last night," says Reesie, as we walk along. "He's gone off to talk to Bobby and his boys today. I told him there was no point to it, but he's a dog with a bone, now that you've put the thought in his head they might have done something to Tricia. I'd like to keep him out of this as much as we can, though."

"No problem," I say.

"He hasn't been the same since your sister disappeared. I didn't know what was wrong at the time." She can't help but let a little irritation slip into her voice. "But a lot of things make sense now."

A part of me is annoyed that Jamie didn't launch his own investigation when Pat disappeared, but now that it's my mission, I'm not sure how I feel about accepting his help. I definitely don't feel like commiserating with his loss, since Pat's *not* dead, just missing. But what will happen when I do find her? Will she go back to Jamie? Will this be just a bump in the road to their happily-ever-after and I'll still be left without my sister? I know I'll be grateful to find her, no matter where she decides to spend the rest of her life, but I'm honest enough to admit I'd like her to be closer to home.

"I just think it's best we don't give Jamie any more false hope till we know where things stand," Reesie continues. "No point opening the wound again."

"Sure," I agree.

After ten minutes, mostly straight uphill, we reach the police station, which sits on the edge of a soccer field. It's a long, two-story wooden building with what are likely bedrooms on the second floor, judging from the freshly laundered sheets fluttering from the railing. It looks like nothing more than a rundown hotel or maybe a youth hostel. Like everything in town, it's surrounded by towering trees, both fruiting and flowering, and is strangely picturesque in spite of its peeling yellow paint.

"You best let me do the talking," says Reesie as we cross the packed dirt past a young officer in khaki pants and a gray T-shirt. He doesn't look up from the motorcycle he's tinkering with.

"Luke should talk," argues Zach, scowling at our joined hands. "It's his sister."

"Luke speaks Spanish?" Reesie says.

Zach looks at me hopefully, but I shake my head.

He sighs as we walk through the only open doorway. We enter a cramped, cluttered room furnished with several desks, filing cabinets and a low table laden with cups and a thermos. A paunchy middle-aged man is sitting behind a desk. A younger officer has pulled up a metal folding chair beside him and they're both glued to a TV show, which I would almost swear is the same one my mom tunes into every day, except that the characters are all speaking Spanish. Neither officer so much as glances in our direction.

"Hola," says Reesie, louder than necessary.

The older man, obviously the one in charge, gives Reesie a cool look. It occurs to me she probably dealt with him last night. He looks none too happy to see her back again so soon. Reluctantly, he stands up and meanders around to our side of the desk. The young guy barely glances up from the program as Reesie and his boss start talking. The exchange goes on for quite a while. Zach shoots me quizzical looks, but I have no more idea what they're saying than he does. Finally, they seem to reach some kind of conclusion and the guy disappears into a back room.

"He just repeated what was in the report about where they found Tricia's clothes," Reesie explains. "I asked him to get them for us. I explained you were her brother."

"They still have her clothes?" I ask, surprised.

"They were holding on to them as evidence, but I got him to see they should hand them over since they're not looking for her anymore."

I stifle an angry comment about how easily they gave up. "You speak good Spanish," I say.

"We go to school in Spanish. In Honduras, the Bay Islanders have always been English-speaking because the islands were settled by British Caymanians. The government wants to change that though. Classes in our schools used to be taught in English, but that's not allowed anymore."

"So do they have any suspects in Pat's disappearance?"

"No. According to them, your sister drowned and the investigation is closed. They're just waiting for her body to come ashore so they can tie up the paperwork." Reesie reaches out and squeezes my hand, but I feel as if I've been punched in the gut. I can't breathe, and the heat is suddenly unbearable. I look longingly out the open doorway.

The officer comes back with shorts and a T-shirt. My heart starts pounding when I recognize the shirt. It was one of Pat's favorites from when she was a swim instructor at our neighborhood pool. She loved the logo on the back, with dolphins swimming through it. Even more, she loved the memory of a job where she got to brainwash unsuspecting kids with her aquatic obsessions. The officer hands Reesie the clothes, then turns to me and says what sounds like an apology.

"He says sorry for your loss," translates Reesie.

I mumble insincere thanks. It burns me that they gave up on Pat like so much flotsam, not even questioning the likelihood of her floating out to sea.

"What was the weather like on the night she disappeared?"
I ask.

Reesie asks the officer, who scowls but walks over to a
filing cabinet behind his desk. He mumbles something to the
other officer, who shoots us an unfriendly look. The older
guy pulls out a thin file and returns to us. I'm not sure whether
to be impressed or skeptical at how quickly he locates it.

"Not a lot of crime here?" I ask.

"Difficult to do wrong when everyone knows everyone
else's business. I imagine that was why your sister chose
McCrae's dock. He closes the place up in the summer, visits
his relations in America, and there's no one else living too
close by."

My stomach plummets as I realize Reesie is assuming Pat
did disappear off McCrae's dock, but then I remember she's
still getting up to speed on a lot of facts about my sister. I
want to set her straight right away. I start to say something,
but the officer clears his throat. He's now standing in front
of us with an open file, which he reads aloud to Reesie.

"He's saying it was a calm night, with a light drizzle early
on that didn't amount to much. There was wave action from
the tides but no wind, so there wouldn't have been much
undertow."

"So how can they believe she drowned?" I demand.

"It's in the report that she'd been drinking."

"Even so, my sister practically lived in the water. If she
was sober enough to walk all the way to McCrae's dock,
how could they think she was so drunk, she'd drown on a
calm night?"

Reesie hesitates, not meeting my eyes.

"Shark?" I ask.

She nods, her eyes misting up. "Sharks have pretty much disappeared from Utila — partly from people finning them, even though it's illegal — but we still do get the occasional hammerhead and reef shark. We've even had a couple of tiger shark sightings, though not so close to shore as she would have been swimming."

I try to think of something else to ask. The drowning explanation doesn't satisfy me, and a shark attack is just too horrific to contemplate. As Reesie said, sharks are uncommon, particularly near shore, so I don't see why that's any more likely than drowning. But it's obvious the police aren't going to reopen the case unless I produce proof of some other explanation.

"What about the drug runners?" I ask. "They know Pat was on the wrong side of them."

Reesie has an exchange with the officer that involves long questions from Reesie and extremely curt responses from the officer. Reesie persists but finally seems satisfied and winds up the interrogation.

"He said they've been keeping a close eye on the drug runners all along, including Bobby's crew, so there's no way they could have gotten away with doing something to Tricia."

"Do you believe them?"

"It's a small island. People don't have a lot to talk about. It is hard to believe anyone local could have got away with a crime like that and kept it a secret."

I try to hide my disappointment, but I think we're all feeling the same as we slump out of the station and past the guy still working on his bike.

"Can I carry her clothes?" asks Zach.

It seems an odd desire, but I hand them over. We walk in silence, making our way back along the same roads and footpaths toward the center of town. I take Reesie's hand this time and try to enjoy just being with her, but I can't get the idea of a shark attack out of my head. It doesn't help that every time I look over at Zach, he's burying his face in my sister's clothes.

"Dude." I stop walking. "Are you sniffing Tricia's clothes?"

He looks from me to Reesie, his face flushed with guilt.

"Buddy," I say more gently, "even though you liked her, that's kind of gross."

"You should pay her more respect," adds Reesie.

"Sorry," Zach mumbles.

"It's okay," I say. "Just don't do it again."

He nods and we resume our journey. I keep an eye on him for a while. A motorcycle whizzing past distracts me, giving me an excuse to pull Reesie out of the way and closer to me. Zach seizes the chance to shove his face in Pat's clothes again. I begin to wonder if he's doing it to bug me. He has to know he's crossing a line.

"Zach!" I lunge toward him, unintentionally stepping into the path of a cyclist, who swerves just in time.

He immediately drops the clothes to his side.

"Haven't you got any more sense than a he-dog?" demands Reesie. "You don't sniff a lady's garments. It's not proper."

"They're not hers," he says quietly.

"What?" I ask.

"These aren't her clothes."

"I'm sorry, buddy, but you're wrong." He's obviously in some weird grief-induced denial. "Those are definitely her clothes."

"No." Zach vigorously shakes his head.

I look at Reesie for support, but she just sighs.

"That boy's sailing with his ship half-rigged. He's always been like this."

"Smell," says Zach earnestly, proffering the clothes.

"Dude," I step back. "I'm not sniffing my sister's clothes."

To my surprise, Reesie takes them and puts them up to her nose. She sniffs, looks at Zach, who nods encouragement, and sniffs again.

"The boy is right," she says in awe. "These may be Tricia's clothes but she definitely was not wearing them the night she went missing. The only thing they smell of is soap, and there's no way a girl could walk that distance to McCrae's dock on a still night and not have B.O. on her clothes."

"She smelled of lemon and strawberries," says Zach indignantly.

"Point remains," says Reesie.

"Any chance the police washed her clothes?" I ask her.

"They wouldn't do that. It would be tampering with evidence."

We start walking again, pondering the question on all of our minds. If Pat wasn't wearing those clothes, then someone put them on that dock. But who would do that, and why?

"If someone hurt Tricia, they might put the clothes on the dock to make it look like a drowning," I say slowly.

"The distress call," says Zach, picking up on my train of thought.

"What're you boys talking about?" asks Reesie.

We fill her in on the little we know as we head for the

Spiny Starfish to see if Mini Mike can add anything to what he told Zach last night.

The Spiny Starfish is hopping with lunchtime customers, and the only available tables are at the far end of the pier in the direct sunlight. The sun hasn't lessened its power since we started up the hill to the police station, so we decide to stand in the shade by the bar. Ten minutes later we're still waiting, as Mini Mike rushes past us with pizzas and beers. My stomach rumbles so we give in and take a seat on the deck. It turns out there's a strong breeze off the water, so we get to enjoy the illusion of coolness while soaking up cancer rays. Mini Mike appears with menus almost immediately, which makes me wonder why he couldn't have taken a minute to speak to us earlier.

"Hey, Zach." Mini Mike claps him on the shoulder. "Don't see you here much in the daytime. Can I get you a beer?"

"No." Reesie butts in before Zach can answer. "We're here for information."

"I want pizza," says Zach, eyeing Reesie to see if she's going to object to that as well.

She looks at me for support, but I shrug.

"Fine," she says. "I suppose we don't have anything more important to do than sit around filling our gullets."

"Share a pepperoni?" I ask Zach. He nods gratefully and I turn to Mini Mike. "We were wondering if there was anything else you could tell us about the distress call the night Tricia disappeared," I say, as I hand back the menu.

"It came in around midnight from the Shark Center. Whoever was on the radio didn't identify himself, but it was a guy who said there'd been an accident. He was putting the call out to anyone who could locate Dr. Dan. Of course, that time of night, everyone knows he'd be at one bar or another. Mind you, even three sheets to the wind, he's one hell of an emergency surgeon. Point is, it took awhile to track him down, and by the time he got to the Shark Center, there was no one around. No one gave it another thought. Kids get up to mischief on the radio all the time."

"Did anyone tell the police?" Reesie asks sharply.

"Don't think so," says Mini Mike, frowning. "I didn't even make the connection until I got to talking to Dr. Dan about Tricia's brother coming around with questions. We really thought it was a prank. The kids often do that," he says with a worried frown.

"Did Dr. Dan even look around to see if someone was hurt?" I try not to sound accusatory. I know all too well how easy it is to see what you should have done after it's too late.

Mini Mike shifts in front of me, momentarily blocking the harsh glare of the sun.

"He didn't find your sister, Luke. He looked everywhere at the time. There was no one there."

I exhale and turn away to stare at the endless miles of ocean. Feeling a hand on my arm, I turn to meet Reesie's warm gaze.

"There is one more thing," says Mini Mike. "I don't know if it's important, but I talked to my girls who were working that night. They said all the shark kids were sitting together early in the evening but one of the girls, not your sister, left in a bit of a huff after some kind of argument. Your sister followed soon after, and the boy was with her."

"Pete?" I demand, feeling like my head is going to explode. "Pete left with my sister?"

"That's right," says Mini Mike. "Does that help?"

I stand up. "I have to go."

"But what about pizza?" groans Zach. "I'm starving."

"You'll live," snaps Reesie. "Now get your backside out of that chair."

"You should have at least let me order a beer," Zach grumbles, trailing us off the deck. "It's made from wheat, you know."

"Really? That's very interesting," Reesie retorts, rushing to keep up with me as I stride through the restaurant. "I'll keep it in mind next time you're vomiting it all over your bedroom floor."

I don't listen to the rest of their arguing as I hit the street and break into a run. I feel like I'm moving in slow motion trying to dodge ambling tourists and whizzing motorbikes. I bump into several people, dimly aware of outraged exclamations. I don't even notice the truck lumbering straight for me. Only Zach's firm hand on my arm, yanking me out of the way at the last minute, saves me from getting flattened. Reesie races forward to cover my other flank. People leap out of our way as we barrel on.

We're at the Shark Center in minutes. I rush into the office, accusations ready to pour out of me, until I see there's no one there. I walk straight past the counter and through the door to the back office, but it's also empty.

"The dock," says Zach, but I'm already out the back door and heading for the boat.

CHAPTER 16

Fully loaded, with at least a dozen divers, the boat is just pulling away from the dock when I emerge from the Shark Center. I sprint, with Reesie and Zach right behind me, and in the heat of the moment one of them shouts something like, "Halt, in the name of the law!"

One guess which one that is.

Pete looks at us, climbs onto the gunwale of the boat, grabs the last rope securing them and, for a nanosecond, I think he's going to hold the boat till we get there. But in a fluid maneuver that he's no doubt done a million times, he slips the knot and pushes the boat out, giving me a three-finger salute, the cool-guy's kiss-off.

"Freeze!" screams Zach.

"Get back here this instant!" adds Reesie.

I hit the dock at warp speed and leap into the growing space between solid wood and receding fiberglass. In midair it occurs to me where I'm going to land if I miss. I hear a splash at the same moment I thump onto the deck. I'm the only one not craning over the side of the boat, so it doesn't take long to find Zach bobbing in the water, looking surprisingly calm.

"Dude, throw me a rope." He waves both arms and begins swimming after us with a speed I wouldn't have thought him capable of.

Reesie, who's still safely on the dock, throws him a life buoy, which he ignores. I make eye contact with Reesie, and she shrugs helplessly as the boat chugs away. I hurl the rope used to tie the boat up. Zach grabs it and hangs on while we continue to motor out to sea. Someone, not Pete or Tracy, shouts up to the captain to stop the boat. Pete and Tracy are leaning over the side like everyone else but they're glaring at Zach. He smiles and waves.

"Hang on, buddy," I shout, trying to keep the panic out of my voice as the coral disappears from under him and the water turns a darker, sinister blue.

"No hurry," he calls back lazily, wrapping the rope around one fist and lying out full length with one arm extended as we drag him along like bait.

"What's going on here?" Dr. Jake appears from the motor room. I wonder who's driving this tub, but I seem to be the only one worrying. Half the divers and Tracy cheerfully fill him in.

I start pulling on our end of the rope, but Zach must have taken on water because I barely gain a foot of rope before I think my hands are going to drop off.

I shout for help, but it seems a detailed explanation of how Zach got on the end of the rope is necessary before anyone can think of rescuing him. After an eternity, or about the time it would take three great whites and a hammerhead to sniff out snack food, Dr. Jake gives the order. A couple of brawny guys in wetsuits leap forward to give me a hand.

Pete still doesn't help. He may be hoping I'll get dragged over the side myself. Tracy, on the other hand, launches into spirited cheerleader mode, shouting encouragement to me and my muscled assistants, because it really is all about teamwork. Only when Zach's head appears over the side of the boat does Pete step forward to grab Zach under his arms and heave him over the side. The force sends him airborne, past the bench, and headfirst onto the deck. I can't help but wonder if it's a last-ditch effort to finish him off. Zach lies still for several moments, gasping like a beached fish.

"You okay, buddy?" I crouch down to help him up onto a bench.

"Cosmic," Zach wheezes, giving me a thumbs-up before putting his head between his knees.

"So you decided to swim with the sharks after all," says Pete, looming above where I'm crouched at Zach's side.

"You could say that." I straighten up and turn to face him. We're almost touching in the narrow space between the fully loaded benches.

"You're not scared anymore?" asks Tracy, who's taken a seat across from Zach.

"Nope," I say, not shifting my gaze from Pete.

"You're the one who should be scared," says Zach.

"Whatever," says Pete, looking from Zach to me and turning away like he's already bored.

He hops up on the bench that runs along the middle of the boat and holds up his hand like he's marshaling a huge unruly crowd instead of a small group of divers seated quietly along the sides.

"How many of you have cameras?" He looks around at the group. Several hold up their hands.

"Well, today we're going to learn to identify sharks."

"Thanks," I say loudly. "I've already got that covered."

"I want you to photograph every whale shark you see today, particularly behind the gills. Then we'll use our computer program to identify individual sharks by their spot patterns." He pauses for the requisite oohs and aahs from the shark lovers. "We also want pictures of scars. As much as spots, scars make every animal wonderfully unique."

"Glad to hear you like scars," I say.

Tracy looks at me quizzically, but Pete continues as if he hasn't heard.

"Whale sharks are highly migratory. The same shark can turn up in locations thousands of miles apart, but no matter where it goes, it can always be identified because its spots never change."

"It's not the only one."

"You have nothing to fear from the sharks."

"Ha!"

Finally, he stops talking and gives me his signature cool-jock stare. I stare right back.

He blinks. "Have you got something to say to me, Luke?" His eyes shift nervously from me to Tracy and back again.

"I think you're the one with something to tell me, Pete." I glance at Tracy just in time to see a look pass between them.

"I don't know what you're talking about."

"I know you were with my sister the night she disappeared."

The divers listen politely, wondering how this fits into their presentation.

"You can't prove a thing."

"I know you reported an emergency the night she disappeared. What did you do to her?"

"Shark!" someone shrieks

"You got that right," I agree.

"GO, GO, GO," shouts Pete, scuttling along the center bench and scooping a mask and snorkel from a bucket at the back. He doesn't bother to put them on before doing a perfect swan dive into an ocean frothing with fish.

I race to the back, knocking over divers right and left, who are suddenly all out of their seats. I snatch a mask and snorkel from the bucket.

"SHARK, SHARK, SHARK," rings out the chorus behind.

"YES, YES!" I shout back, not pausing to think as I vault the back railing, hitting what must be the diving ledge. Teetering there, still clutching a mask and snorkel, I suddenly remember where I am and sink down onto the small platform, watching Pete splash out of reach. I feel a moment of relief when the other divers swarm past me to chase him.

But then I see it.

Its dorsal fin crests a good four feet above the water as it does a lazy arc around the boat. Every inch of it is visible in the horrifyingly clear Caribbean Sea. Roughly twice the length of our boat, it floats alongside as if it's doing a little reconnaissance before moving in for the kill. It has to know how easily it could take us down. One well-placed bump and we'd be miles offshore, in thousands of feet of ocean, just waiting to be someone's dinner.

As it reaches the front of the boat, it angles away, swimming more quickly but with an economy of movement, its massive tail sweeping back and forth, barely disturbing the surface of the water. Pete, now followed by a posse of like-minded nut-jobs who, it turns out, were not trying to apprehend him after all, snorkel after it with a good deal more splashing and noise. Only when it's led them half a mile from the boat does it dive into the crystal depths. I watch in disbelief as they swim sadly in circles, bobbing and diving, seeking one last glimpse, not even considering their own precarious situation. I notice Zach is among them, which doesn't really surprise me. He's one of the converted, just like my sister.

I relax on my perch and wait for the crazies to give up and return to safety. Looking at the vast watery wasteland, I try to imagine what it would be like to enjoy the rocking of a boat on a sparkling ocean under a cobalt sky. Pat spent weeks doing exactly what I'm doing now, although technically she was in the water and close to the shark instead of a sensible distance away. I try to imagine that our spirits are closer as I experience what she must have felt so many times. I'm seeing what she saw, feeling what she felt. I close my eyes for a moment, letting her spirit wash over me, which totally explains what happens next, not to mention the indisputable truth that communing with spirits is a bad idea.

I open my eyes to discover the massive killing machine has snuck up on me. Its wide gaping mouth that could effortlessly swallow a guy four times my size bursts from the water inches from my dangling feet.

ME: *This is so your fault.*
PAT: *He likes you.*

ME: *Of course he does. He's probably hungry.*

PAT: *You see it, don't you?*

ME: *My impending death? Yeah, I see it.*

PAT: *It's the largest fish in the sea. It could swallow you whole.*

ME: *Thanks for that tidbit of wisdom. I can see why you wanted to introduce people to the joys of whale sharks. You're a real natural.*

PAT: *And yet it won't.*

ME: *Won't what?*

PAT: *You know. You can see it in its eyes.*

I look more closely at the rubbery gray maw bobbing inches beneath my feet. Obviously, it must be looking at me, but from this angle all I see is mouth.

ME: *I can't see its eyes.*

PAT: *You haven't pulled your legs up.*

ME: *What?*

PAT: *Because you know it won't hurt you.*

ME: *You're delusional.*

PAT: *Am I?*

ME:

"It's back at the boat!" The cry rings out from the distant thrashing disciples, who think this wild, star-speckled creature is there for their entertainment. They race toward it, practically drowning each other in their haste, but the beast is in no hurry. It watches me a few moments longer, then arches its back, its dorsal briefly cutting the water, does a graceful flip and disappears into the depths. Its departure is effortless and final. There's no negotiation, no last chance to say good-bye, no way of understanding why it chose to hang out at all or why it left when it did.

"Where is it?" asks the first of the divers to reach the boat, struggling out of his flippers and handing them up to me so he can climb the ladder.

"Gone."

"Aw, darn, did you get a good look at it?"

"No, it disappeared too quickly. I don't think I ever really saw it at all."

The guy gives me an odd look as he swings onto the dive platform and clambers over the back of the boat. I stay where I am and help successive divers, until Tracy shows up to relieve me. Pete takes his time leaving the water, making a show of being a gentleman, letting everyone go ahead of him.

I move to a bench, where Zach joins me. "It was so awesome," he crows. "You should have seen it, man. It was like mega-huge and it was covered in freaking remoras all over its head, and the mouth was like . . ." He chatters on but I stop listening.

ME: *Is that it?*

PAT: *What?*

ME: *You saw that every day. The beauty, the total freedom. Is that what it felt like to be free of us?*

PAT: *You're free now. You don't have to go back. What's it like for you?*

ME:

For the next several hours, the same scene plays out over and over. We find one. The divers explode into its world, chase and harass it, only to lose it when it's had enough of them. I don't try to talk to Pete. I want answers, but for now my questions have nothing to do with the night Pat disappeared or his involvement. Even if he did something to her — and I will get to the truth of that — he can't be anything more than the end of a story that I need to understand from the beginning.

The sun is low on the horizon when we finally head in. Reesie, solid and motionless, is sitting on the dock where we left her, waiting. She stands up and catches the rope Pete throws, tying up the boat with the easy efficiency of the island-born.

"So do you want me to call the police now?" she asks, loud enough for Pete to hear, as he jumps off the boat and reaches up for the equipment I start to off-load. Zach joins Pete on the dock and starts ferrying equipment to the Shark Center, while Dr. Jake and Tracy help the divers collect their gear and go through the well-rehearsed routine of trying to sign them up for future trips.

"What's this about police?" asks Dr. Jake after the last of the tourists is out of earshot.

"Pete knows something about my sister's disappearance," I say wearily. I want answers, but I'm no longer so certain he's the one who can give them to me.

"I don't know what he's talking about," asserts Pete without conviction. The hours on the boat have given us all time to think. Maybe he's tired of lying.

"He's talking about you making a distress call the night his sister went missing," says Reesie.

"Sorry, I can't help you." He turns away, his eyes on the horizon, where the sun is dropping into the sea.

"People saw you leave with her," insists Zach.

"They know it was you who made that call," says Reesie. We exchange glances. Like me, she's felt the shift in him.

"I don't know what happened," he croaks. I realize, to my absolute amazement, that he's crying and I almost feel sorry for him.

"It's okay, Pete," says Tracy earnestly. "We need to tell them the truth now."

CHAPTER 17

r. Jake insists we all go into the office and sit down. He sends Tracy across the road for cold drinks, so minutes later, I'm relaxing on an overstuffed sofa sipping a cold one. Zach and Reesie are flanking me on either side while I wait for my sister's attacker to finally spill his guts. He's taking his time, sitting where Dr. Jake has placed him in a straight-backed chair across the room. Dr. Jake has pulled up another chair for himself an equal distance between us. Tracy is hovering in the doorway. She could bring in a chair from the outer room but doesn't.

"Tell us what happened, son," Dr. Jake prompts.

The kindness in his voice reminds me that he and Pete have history. He hired him, trusted him, probably respected him. But he cared about my sister as well. I have to believe he'll make sure she gets justice.

Pete exhales, takes a long drag on his cigarette, a slug of his beer, and stares at a point just beyond me. I wonder if he can feel Pat's presence in the room like I do.

"I wanted her from the first time I saw her," he begins.

Reesie reaches for my hand, which is already curling into a fist.

"She seemed like she might be interested at first. We flirted at work, but I could never get past first base. It was like she was always waiting for someone better to come along."

"An egotistical, smart-ass jock not good enough for her; that's hard to figure," I interject.

"The night she disappeared, I thought maybe I was finally going to get my shot."

"I thought you and Tracy were dating," says Dr. Jake, looking confused.

Tracy's mouth twists before she forces a good-natured smile.

"We were never serious," she says.

"The minute Tricia met your brother, it was game over for me," continues Pete, glancing at Reesie. "But that night, the night she disappeared, she and Jamie had a fight and she came to me for comfort. I told her he wasn't good enough for her."

I feel Reesie start to rise, and I'm glad I'm still holding her hand as I gently pull her back.

"I bought her a few drinks. Everything was going well. Then, suddenly, out of nowhere, she wants to go back to her room."

He stops and turns his attention to his beer, knocking back the dregs and leaning over to place the bottle on the ground. Tracy darts forward, takes his bottle and simultaneously hands him another. I wonder how many she's got. I could use another one myself.

"What did you do next?" I ask.

"I walked her back."

Pausing, he gulps his beer. I barely resist the urge to snatch his bottle and smash it over his head. Instead, I squeeze Reesie's hand and feel a little calmer when she squeezes mine back.

"We went down to the dock. We were both pretty drunk. She said she wanted to be alone, but girls always say that, don't they?"

"Sure," I agree, "when assholes are hitting on them and they want to be left alone."

I can see the fear in his eyes. The end is near.

For both of us.

"I tried to kiss her," he says quickly, rushing to get it over with. "We struggled. It was an accident. She pulled away too hard and fell. She hit her head on the side of the boat."

I suck in air, starting to hyperventilate as my mind races. This is the information I've been waiting so long for, but it's not what I wanted to hear. A million questions flood my brain. How badly was she hurt? Why wasn't she there when Dr. Dan showed up? Where is she now?

I'm vaguely aware of Reesie's hand, wrapped around mine like a vise. She thinks she's holding me back, but it's an unnecessary precaution. I feel weak, picturing my sister in pain, bleeding, on the very same dock I've walked out on every day since I've been here. I'm not even sure I could stand up, much less launch an attack. How could I have been so close and not notice anything? Is her blood still there, soaked into the planks? The thought causes cold beads of sweat to pop out on my forehead. I'm frozen in anticipation of what Pete's going to disclose next. Zach, however, is not.

He ricochets off the sofa, knocking Pete to the ground before any of us has time to react.

"I'll kill you!" Zach screams, pummeling Pete in the head, tears streaming down his face. "How could you treat her like that?" He punctuates each word with a volley of fists. "You" pow "had" pow, pow "no right," bam, smash, thwack. "Do you hear me, you bastard?!"

Finally, I'm spurred to action. I leap off the sofa and grab Zach from behind, pulling him off Pete. It's not that I wouldn't like to beat the guy myself, but I need to hear the end of the story. Zach collapses against me, panting and sobbing. Reesie joins us on the floor and puts an arm around him, rubbing his back. Eventually he quiets down and we return our attention to Pete, who's moved to the sofa and is stretched out, groaning. Blood trickles from his nose and I can see the beginning of swelling under one eye, though he's covering most of his face with his arm and is half-shielded by Dr. Jake, who's perched on the edge of the sofa guarding him.

I stand up, towering over him. "What happened next?"

His voice is a hoarse croak. "I called for help."

"Should I call Dr. Dan?" asks Tracy.

"In a minute," says Dr. Jake. "Where was Tricia when you called for help, Pete?"

"I left her on the dock." His voice is barely above a whisper. Even I'm starting to think Tracy should go for help, but how much help did this asshole give my sister?

"How badly was she hurt?" says Dr. Jake, voicing my thoughts.

"Bad, but she was conscious. There was a lot of blood. I left her, but I was going to go back for her. I just needed to radio for help."

He struggles to sit up. "You have to believe me. I radioed for help. As soon as I got word Dr. Dan was on his way, I went back to sit with her but she was gone. I thought she must have headed back to her room, but when I checked, Tracy was there alone."

"He told me what happened," Tracy confirms in a small voice. "I'm so sorry I didn't tell you, but it wouldn't have made any difference. She was gone. We looked everywhere for her — back at the Spiny Starfish and even up at Jamie's house. We thought maybe she'd gone looking for him. That would have been natural. We didn't have the nerve to knock on his door, it was so late. If we'd known where she was going . . ." She stops, her voice cracking as tears roll down her face. She slides down the wall to the floor, burying her head in folded arms, quietly sniveling.

I turn from Tracy to Pete, slumped back on the sofa, his eyes closed.

"How could she get all the way across town, bleeding? Why would she do that?" I demand.

"I dunno," murmurs Pete, his mouth barely moving. "I've asked myself that a million times. Maybe she was upset about the fight with Jamie. Maybe . . ." He stops.

"Maybe what, Pete?" says Dr. Jake.

He exhales loudly. "Maybe she was hiding from me." His voice cracks. "Maybe she thought I was going to come back and hurt her and she was trying to get as far away from me as she could. I never would have thought to look for her on McCrae's dock. Even if I walked from one end of town to the other, it would never have occurred to me to check there. And Tricia, if she was scared, really scared, she'd want to be near the ocean."

"You're lying," moans Zach. "You killed her and now you're trying to cover it up. Don't believe him, Luke."

I sure as hell don't want to believe any of this, but Pete's not the same guy he was an hour ago. The swagger's gone, and not just because Zach beat it out of him.

ME: *Is this the way it happened, Pat?*

PAT: *Does he seem like he's lying?*

ME:

"Call the doctor, Tracy, and the police," says Dr. Jake. "I'm sorry, Luke. I wish it was better news."

"She wouldn't drown. Tricia couldn't drown," insists Zach.

"She was hurt," says Dr. Jake. "If she was disoriented, maybe she fell in the water, and if she was bleeding, in the water at night . . ."

My breath catches in my throat as I finish that sentence in my head. "But isn't there a chance she just wandered off and got lost?" I ask.

"It's a small island, Luke. Someone would have seen her by now."

Suddenly my vision is flooded with an image of tangled hair, a gaping eye socket. My ears pound with the steady rhythm of . . . what? What is it I'm hearing? So familiar. Like breathing. I hunker down on the floor, giving in to it, trying to remember, to understand.

Reesie's at my side in an instant and Zach with her.

"I'm sorry, man," says Zach but his voice is coming from a distance. I can barely hear him.

Reesie just folds me in her arms, and I cling to her until the vision is gone, until there's nothing but emptiness.

CHAPTER 18

"**S**he drowned just like they said."

I hold the phone away from my ear so I don't have to hear their grief, but it echoes through the handset, reverberating inside me, like defeat.

I promised to bring her home.

I failed.

Again.

"I think she went into the water accidentally," I continue, hoping to give them some peace.

None of us ever admitted our biggest fear — that Pat was so desperate to get away from us, she took her own life.

"She was attacked. The guy who did it has been arrested, but he didn't kill her. That part was an accident."

I move the phone a little closer, in case they want to say something, but it just makes the sobbing more audible. I place the handset on the desk in front of me.

Zach and Reesie sit in silent witness on the couch. Dr. Jake and Tracy have gone to the police station with Pete to give their statements. Later, Dr. Jake will call Pete's family. I don't envy him the call. In the end, Pete was an asshole but not a villain. It's not clear yet whether he'll be charged. The police whom Dr. Jake called to pick him up seemed eager to have someone to blame. The island relies on tourism and they're peaceable people. The death of a teenager is not only bad for business but bad for morale. Pete will lose his job, go home in disgrace and live with what he did to my sister for the rest of his life. He'll pay, one way or another.

"Are you coming home?" asks Mom.

The tiny voice emerging from the headset is both pleading and frightened. I look at it as if it's actually the one speaking, taking a moment to contemplate the possibilities.

PAT: *You could learn how to dive.*

ME: *Unlike you, I don't throw myself into life-threatening situations, remember?*

PAT: *Mini Mike offered you a job.*

ME: *And then what?*

PAT: *You and Reesie . . .*

ME:

I pick up the phone.

"There are a few things to tie up here with the investigation," I stall. "And I've still got a couple of weeks left before school."

"But then you'll come home?" Her voice is thin, hollow, as it crosses a space between us that's too wide to be measured.

I picture her, alone in the kitchen though my father is less than three feet away, her wineglass next to her on the counter, the bottle beside it. She'll be looking out the window at the back garden as she hears my news, watching the birds feed at one of her dozen feeders. Pat isn't the only one who loves wildlife.

I picture my father, slumped over the kitchen table, watching my mother, helpless to take away her grief. He's spent a lifetime trying, but this time it's too much even for him. Maybe, like me, he'll finally realize it's easier not to try so hard.

I swallow.

"I'll be home soon, Mom," I promise. It's all I can do for her.

She asks if I want to speak to my father. I lie and say I do. When he comes on the line, I try to think of something to say that will change the reality of Pat's death. I want to apologize, but I'm not sure why.

"So there's no body?" he asks.

"No."

"And you're sure she's dead?"

"Yeah."

"Are you okay?"

"Yeah."

"Do you need money?"

"No."

"I love you, Luke."

It's a sucker punch, but I take it like a man, breathing slowly in and out.

"I love you, too, Dad. How's Mom?"

"You know. She's taking it hard."

"I need to get going now."

"Right, of course." He's suddenly awkward. "Do you need anything?"

"No, I'm okay."

I notice Reesie and Zach watching me, listening to every word. How much can they understand from hearing just my end of it? Zach gives me two thumbs-up. Reesie crosses the room, leans on the arm of my chair and puts her hand on my shoulder, looking into my eyes with the promise of her world, where love doesn't come packaged with disappointment.

"I'll call again in a few days," I say. Not waiting for his reply, I replace the receiver and stare at it for a few minutes in silence.

"Parents — who needs them?" Zach blusters, but I see pain in his eyes.

"It'll work out," says Reesie.

"Go for a beer?" asks Zach.

I hesitate. I can't imagine a situation where I'd have a better excuse to get hammered, but that's just what it is. An excuse. A cop-out. A way to block out the reality that Pat's gone and she's never coming back.

"I think I may lay off for a while," I say, hoping I don't sound preachy.

Zach scowls at Reesie like she's responsible. "I'll be at the Spiny Starfish if you change your mind."

He looks so broken as he trudges out of the room that I almost go after him, but as much as I feel like I'm betraying him, dulling my pain would betray Pat.

PAT: *So is this the new you?*

ME: *Isn't that what you always wanted?*

PAT: *It's a little late, don't you think?*

ME:

"We should tell Jamie." Reesie breaks into my thoughts.

It's an effort to stand up, put one foot in front of the other. The mechanics of motion, breathing, moving forward, are no longer automatic. I'm grateful when Reesie takes my hand.

———

The walk up the hill to her house seems to have lengthened. I'm surprised it's still daylight. Nanny says something when we let ourselves in through the gate. I register her presence, rocking on their porch swing, but can't make sense of her words. Reesie responds, Nanny hugs me and goes inside. We take her place on the swing, still warm from her body. Donny comes out almost immediately, looks at me with huge eyes and sinks down onto the porch deck.

Nanny reappears with Reesie's mom and two trays laden with tea, Nanny's bread, homemade cookies and mango preserve. There's far too much food for just us. I note every detail and am handed tea and an overflowing plate. Touching neither, I rock with Reesie, back and forth, as she tells the end of Pat's story. More chairs appear and more people. The porch fills with faces I don't know; people spill into the yard as word spreads and the community rallies. Reesie retells the story many times and, each time, her audience listens in silence.

Finally, Jamie appears. It's been dark for what seems like hours, though time has lost all meaning. I feel numb. Nothing seems real. The landscape of sea-weathered people, lush towering trees, hand-hewn furniture on a rickety porch blurs at the edges like a watercolor, too charming for the despair that fills me.

As Jamie walks through the gate, he shimmers in the moonlight. I see the certainty of Pat's death dawn on his face before Reesie says a word. Hands reach out for him as he works his way slowly through the crowd. Someone brings him a chair. He collapses into it under the weight of lost hope. Until that moment, I hadn't realized that he, too, at least half-believed I could bring Pat back. We keep a silent vigil.

Time passes. The crowd thins out, drifts away. I shake many hands, don't hear many words. But they are spoken — offers of sympathy and solidarity. Nanny takes Donny inside, Reesie's mom follows, and as the first cock announces the approaching dawn, Jamie, Reesie and I find ourselves alone.

"It's my fault she left," I say. "My fault she didn't want to come home."

Jamie looks at me. "How can you say that? She loved you, Luke, more than anything, maybe more than she was capable of loving anyone else. You weren't the reason she left."

"You don't understand."

"You let her go, Luke, because it was the right thing to do. As for not wanting to go home — I never met your parents, but the way Trish told it, she always felt like she had to be in control, she could never let loose and be a kid. It was a burden she carried a long time. When she got here, she was ready to set it down, but you weren't ever the burden."

I search his face, wanting badly to believe him. It explains a lot — a new name, new behavior — but it doesn't explain everything.

"I was the one she had to be perfect for, not my parents. It was me she was trying to protect."

"You sure about that? The way she told it, you were the one who always looked out for her."

ME: *Is that what you told him? Why would you lie about me?*

PAT: *What makes you think I was lying?*

"She gave away my necklace," I say dully. "I gave it to her years ago. She never took it off. But she gave it away. I couldn't have been that important to her."

Jamie gapes at me.

"You probably never noticed it," I continue. "Maybe she gave it away before you met her."

"The silver starfish?"

"Yeah."

"What makes you think she gave it away?"

"I saw it. Tracy has it. Pat gave it to her."

"Trish never took that necklace off!" says Jamie vehemently. "You have to believe me, Luke. She told me the whole story of how you saved up for it and what it meant to her. Not to mention the fact that she and Tracy hated each other. Trish had already asked Dr. Jake for a single room. She made it a condition of her staying on permanently."

I examine his face, trying to get some hint that he's just trying to make me feel better, but his confusion is palpable. As the implications of this new information filter through both of our minds, he's angry, too.

"Do you remember if she was wearing the necklace the last night you saw her?" I ask urgently.

"She *always* wore it," he insists, jumping to his feet. "There's something very wrong here, Luke."

All three of us are off the porch in seconds, sprinting out the gate. We don't even need to discuss where we're headed as we career down the hill toward the Shark Center.

CHAPTER 19

Since it's just past dawn, the Shark Center's still locked, but the first person we see as we approach the office is Zach, sitting on the front step. He jumps up when he spots us and runs at me.

"I've been waiting for hours." He clutches my arm. "Where were you? I thought maybe you'd done something crazy."

"I thought *you* were getting drunk. What are you doing here?"

He smiles proudly. "Change of plans, my man. If you're climbing on the sobriety wagon, I'm coming with you. We're brothers, right?"

"Brothers." I nod and hold up my fist, which he bangs with such enthusiasm we both wince.

"I hate to throw water on your party," says Reesie, "but we've got business to attend to."

We head through the broken archway and down the path to the back of the Shark Center, pausing when we discover the equipment room open. There's no sign of Tracy inside so we continue on toward the bedrooms. Reesie fills Zach in on the new information we've pieced together, and Zach confirms that Tracy and Pat didn't get along. He also has his own story about the necklace. He recalls the time when Tracy admired it and asked Pat where she could get one like it.

"She was always doing that," finishes Zach. "She said mean stuff about Tricia behind her back, but she always copied her. It was like she hated Tricia but wanted to *be* Tricia at the same time."

I lead the way to Tracy's room, the one she shared with my sister, but there's no answer when we knock. We debate whether she could still be at the police station. In the middle of our discussion, Reesie turns away from the rooms and spots Tracy out on the dock. She looks tiny, silhouetted against an expanse of blue sky that melts into the postcard-perfect sapphire ocean. We hurry down the path, keeping her in our sight. She's sitting at the end of the dock, sipping a cup of something and swinging her slender suntanned legs over the edge. Next to her is a pile of dive equipment she must have lugged out there herself, since Dr. Jake is unlikely to have arrived this early and she's running out of co-workers. I can't help but be a little amazed. Half a dozen buoyancy control device jackets are neatly stacked next to the tanks, masks, and regulators, all ready for loading. She's either a lot stronger than she looks or very determined to pick up the slack.

As I step onto the dock, she turns and gives a friendly wave. The wind whips her sun-bleached hair across her face, and I'm startled for a moment because there's something profoundly different about her, but it takes me a minute to realize what it is. As I gaze into her clear blue eyes, I'm suddenly struck that she's not just cute anymore. She's downright beautiful, glowing against the breaking dawn. She reaches up to push her hair back, and my eyes are drawn to the sparkle at her throat — my sister's necklace.

She shouts something, but her words, tossed on the wind, are drowned out by the rhythmic pounding of the surf. The dock shudders with each new wave. For a moment I forget what I'm doing here as my mind and body fight to maintain balance and I'm flooded with a feeling of déjà vu.

She flashes her perfect teeth as I approach. I sense the others right behind me. Their expressions must mirror my own because her smile turns to a frown as she looks from one face to another.

"Is something wrong?" she asks, her hand casually reaching up to her throat to finger the shell-inlaid starfish.

I barely resist the urge to yank it off her neck.

Reesie is not so self-restrained. "Where you'd get this?" she demands, swooping down and grabbing up the starfish with a vehemence that surely makes the chain dig into the back of Tracy's neck.

Tears spring to Tracy's eyes as she looks to me for support, but I return her gaze coldly.

"I know my sister didn't give that to you, so you better answer Reesie's question."

A particularly large wave crashes against the dock, knocking us all off balance. Reesie loses her grip on the necklace, giving Tracy just enough time to scramble to her feet, though there are still four of us blocking her way off the dock. She rubs the back of her neck and gives me a reproachful look.

"Why would I lie about it?"

"You tell me."

"Trish didn't even like you." Jamie steps toward her, looming over her. "No way she'd be giving you something as precious as that necklace."

Tracy doesn't flinch under Jamie's penetrating glare, but her eyes flit back and forth to the shoreline.

"Fine," she says finally. "I found it on the dock, the day after she disappeared. It must have come off during her struggle with Pete. I know I shouldn't have kept it." She shoots me an apologetic look. "But I didn't see what difference it would make since she was gone anyway."

"She'd only been *gone* a few hours. What made you so sure she wasn't coming back?" I ask.

"I wasn't sure. If she'd come back, of course I'd have returned it to her."

"You told me you and Pat were friends."

She shrugs. "It was obvious by then she was dead. What good would it have done to tell you your sister was a bitch? I imagine you knew that anyway."

For one second I think I've slapped her, as I hear the thwack and see the redness streak across her cheek. Then I realize Reesie has once again moved in for the kill. I take a second to be grateful she's on my side.

"Don't you dare be speaking ill of his sister," Reesie glowers.

Tracy's eyes glitter, but it's not with tears this time. She glares at me, all hint of softness gone so completely, I wonder if it was ever there at all.

"Do you want to know what it was like living with your sister? Do you really want to know?"

She doesn't give me time to answer as she barrels on.

"From the first day she arrived here, everyone loved her." Her voice is laden with venom. "Pete was *my* boyfriend before she came. We'd been sleeping together for weeks. He broke up with me an hour after he met her, no explanation. He became obsessed with her. And you . . ." she turns on Jamie. "Do you remember we used to flirt?"

Jamie gapes at her.

"You never spoke to me after she got here. It was like I'd suddenly become invisible. Everyone was the same — Dr. Jake, every diver who ever came out on our boat. She bewitched them, but they were too stupid to see it."

"What did you do to her?" Jamie croaks, and I turn to see the horror at Tracy's hatred etched in his face.

"Nothing. That's the best part. My idiot ex-boyfriend finished them both off."

We're all distracted by the drone of a small incoming plane. It glides low over our heads as it dives in to land.

"That will be the police coming for Pete," Tracy says. "Did you hear? They're charging him with attempted murder. So I guess you'll get some justice after all, Luke."

I don't know what to do with this information. Should I feel happy Pete is looking at years in a Honduran jail? I want him punished for what he did to my sister, but he wasn't trying to kill her. Somehow Tracy's overt malice seems almost worse.

"Imagine Pete spending the rest of his life in a Honduran jail," Tracy continues as if reading my mind. "I don't imagine it'll be a very long life, though, given the violence in the local prisons. Now, if you guys will excuse me, he made me promise I'd come see him off. I'm the only friend he has now. Payback's a bitch, isn't it?"

"Someone sure is," says Reesie.

Tracy giggles good-naturedly and, for a moment, she's once again the girl I first met, sweet and vulnerable.

A coldness creeps across my flesh.

No one tries to stop her as she pushes past us and saunters off the dock.

"Do you think Pat had any idea what she was really like?" I ask, looking from one shocked face to another.

Jamie shakes his head sadly. "I hope not."

"I don't get it," says Zach.

"Me, neither," I agree. "That girl takes female jealousy to a whole new level."

"No, not that. . . ."

"What don't you get?" I ask gently.

"Well, she hated Tricia, right?"

"Is he only working that out now?" interrupts Reesie.

"Can't you let the boy have one minute to think?" Jamie shushes her.

"Aren't enough minutes in the day, if that's what we're waiting for," mutters Reesie, but she keeps quiet while we wait for Zach to go on.

Instead he slumps down on the dock and sits cross-legged, playing with the pressure gauge on one of the regulators Tracy has left unattended. It's weird that she just walked away and left this stuff. I guess there's not much theft here because she couldn't have thought we would guard it for her while she said her good-byes to my sister's attacker.

"Tracy hated Pete, and she's happy he got caught," says Zach.

"Thanks for the recap," says Reesie. "We'll be keeping you in mind the next time Nanny misses one of her soaps."

"So why would she help him look for Tricia the night she got lost? And why would she help him cover up what he did?" he persists. "And who left the voodoo dolls? And someone got freshly washed clothes from Tricia's room and planted them on McCrae's dock because those clothes hadn't been worn and they didn't have blood on them."

We stare at him in shocked silence. The coldness that washed over me with Tracy's revelations has seeped into my bones. I don't think it would take more than a stiff wind or one more piece of intel to shatter me. I sink down to the dock and rest my head in my hands, feeling the warmth of Reesie's body as she plumps down next to me. When I look up, I see that Jamie is also sitting, but he's turned away, staring out to sea.

"Well, as I live and breathe," says Reesie finally, her voice soft with admiration. "You still got some brain cells left after all."

"But Pete admitted he hurt my sister," I point out, though I really don't know what to think anymore.

"Pete admitted he left your sister bleeding on the dock," says Reesie. "He doesn't know what happened to her after that."

My stomach starts to pitch like a turbulent sea. I feel every wave that pounds the dock like it's breaking inside me, one after another, a steady rhythm so familiar it's like breathing. I close my eyes, trying to calm my inner tempest, but it only gets worse, and then I see her. Long swirling black hair, her once beautiful face, now bloated and gouged, one eye missing and the other no longer the brilliant green of a tropical forest but the green-gray of seaweed. I open my eyes and look down at the water just in time to catch sight of it. Its star-speckled wings flutter gracefully as it disappears under the dock, only to reappear seconds later, skimming the surface as it heads back out to sea.

Why does it keep returning to this spot?

I know I've found her before my hands touch the water, before it rushes up my nostrils, before the salt stings my eyes. I follow the gathered fish — a long barracuda, its fraggle teeth too big for its sharp pointed jaw, a blotchy-skinned cowfish, a school of disc-shaped blue tang. I can name them all. Pat was right. I always could. We shared a passion, until I realized it was only a matter of time before it would divide us — her need to throw herself at life regardless of the risks, my need to hang back.

My lungs ache as I work my way down to her; my ears feel like they're imploding. I see her eddying hair first and mistake it for something natural, a few fronds of sea grass swaying with the current, sheltering the tiny minnows that flit in and out. Three more strokes and I'm looking into her face, the gaping eye socket every bit as terrifying as in my visions, her open eye even more so. It tracks my every movement as I pull at her, trying to take her with me to the surface. Her head tilts back dangerously. I wonder if the neck could snap, the skin and bone separate, and then, as if in answer to my ghastly question, a chunk of her flesh comes away in my hand, revealing the bare ashen bone of her shoulder. I open my mouth to scream and water rushes in. I choke. Darkness — not unwelcome — overcomes me.

The sea changes from translucent blue to the blackness of an earthen grave as reality and imaginings weave together. It's no longer me grabbing her but her grabbing me. I lash out in horror and scream again, only to find something shoved into my gaping mouth. It's air, not water rushing in. I push it away, strike out, feeling only fear and perhaps resignation. Pat waits for me in the darkness, and I'm ready to join her. But a hand encircles my arm and again the object is shoved into my mouth. As I suck in again, my senses clear. I reach up, close my hand over the mouthpiece of a regulator and look into Zach's face, inches from my own. We thrash about as he works my arms into a BCD, fastens it around my torso and slips a mask over my head. I don't make it easy. Finally successful in forcing me into the equipment, he gives me the thumbs-up. I dimly remember reviewing hand signals with Pat when she was studying for her first dive exam. I answer his question with my own thumbs-up, though I can think of few circumstances when this signal would be more wrong.

In our struggle, Pat has disappeared. I panic, thinking I've lost her, but again I follow the fish that feast on her remains. A school of torpedo-shaped jacks leads us straight to her. I look back at Zach, see the horror in his face as his eyes widen and bubbles rise too fast from his own respirator. I point to her hair, try to show him the problem, and his dive training takes over as he moves in, methodically running his fingers through her locks searching for the snag. He dives deeper and shifts her body, and suddenly we can both see where her hair has caught on a cable securing a joint in the dock. He pulls at the strand of hair, looking at me helplessly as it refuses to

CHAPTER 20

In the end, we drag Pat out of the water, weight belt and all. It takes Jamie, Reesie and Zach all pulling from above and me pushing from below to heave her waterlogged body onto the dock. I'm the one who stays in the water and gets a firm grip on her butt to hoist her up. I won't let Zach help me. It's the only dignity I can offer her in a death that's stripped her of everything else.

When we finally have her resting faceup, looking at the sky for the first time in weeks, no one can figure out what to do next. The shock of her, finally among us, is too enormous. I take her hand. There's nothing of my sister in its slimy coldness but a lot of the horror she endured. I tell myself she wasn't conscious when she went into the water, but I know that's a lie. I've seen her struggle. I've heard her screams. They've filled my dreams as her teasing voice once filled my waking hours.

Jamie has left the dock, Reesie with him. They're standing together on the shore, turned away from us. I can tell he's crying, though no sound reaches me. I envy him the easy release of his grief, the sister steadfast at his side, the last weeks he spent with Pat, weeks I lost. Zach is several feet away, on his hands and knees, leaning over the side of the dock puking his guts out. My eyes fill with tears of rage — at my sister, her murderer and most of all myself.

ME: *It's all my fault.*

PAT:

ME: *But I had to make you leave, Pat. You understand that, don't you? You and Mom were tearing each other apart, and you were starting to lose hope. Do you remember when you said you might defer your scholarship and stay home another year? I couldn't let you do that.*

PAT:

I peer into her cold, fish-gray eye. It stares back without forgiveness.

ME: *I know I screwed up, but you have to believe I did it for you.*

PAT:

"We need to get the police," says Zach tonelessly. I didn't notice him approach and glance up to find him standing above us, his head sunk into his hunched shoulders, his gaze off to the side. "I'll go, if you want to stay with her."

I look up at him, shielding my eyes against the blistering sun, and try to make sense of what he's saying — something about the police. It's too late for the police. Doesn't he see that? I turn back to my sister. Sweat drips off my face, mingling with the salt water on hers. Together they form rivulets sliding across her cheeks like tears. I take her hand again. It's still the clammy, foreign object it was before, but I force myself not to let go.

ME: *Say something, Pat. Please, just say something.*

PAT:

"Luke." I start as Reesie touches my arm. I look back at the shore. Jamie's no longer in sight. Nor is Zach. "Dr. Jake is back from seeing Pete off on the plane. He's calling the police now."

"What about Tracy?"

Reesie's brow furrows. "You want to talk to Tracy? I didn't see her. Maybe she went back to her room."

I stand up and stride off the dock, breaking into a run when I hit dry land. I race to the office, stop just inside the door and take in the scene. Zach, Jamie and Dr. Jake are there, talking in hushed tones, but there's no sign of Tracy.

"Where's Tracy?" I demand, my voice tight.

Dr. Jake looks at me in surprise. "I don't know. I haven't seen her since early this morning. We have a dive going out later. She said she was going to get some gear ready, but maybe she went back to bed."

"She wasn't at the airport seeing Pete off?" Zach asks, but it comes out as a more of a statement as comprehension blooms on his face.

I'm out the door before Dr. Jake can reply. As my feet pound the cement walkway to Tracy's room, Zach is on my heels. I bang on the door. Zach leans past me, turns the knob and throws it open. We rush in and freeze as we take in the scene in front of us. The room is empty. Tracy's clothes, her Hello Kitty toiletry bag, her backpack, all gone.

"It was her," I stare at the deserted room that chides me with the evidence that once again I've failed.

"We'll find her," says Zach.

"How? She's gone; she could be anywhere. We'll never find her."

"This is Utila," says a voice behind Zach. Reesie pushes past him into the room. "We just need to get ourselves on the radio. There's no place to hide."

Together we hurry back to the office. Dr. Jake meets us at the door. By the mixture of revulsion and concern on his face, I know he and Jamie have already figured out what's going on.

"Was she there?" Jamie asks grimly.

"We need the radio," says Reesie.

Dr. Jake points at it and sinks down on the couch, his head in his hands. We brush past him, and Jamie joins us as we huddle around the radio. I fidget while Reesie flips it on and repeatedly punches a button, flicking through stations.

"I'm tuning in to the emergency frequency," she explains. "There're some people always on standby on it. It's the fastest way to get the word out. After that, we can try individual stations, track her down when we start getting some sightings."

Jamie takes the mike out of her hands and pushes down the button, speaking into it hoarsely. "Putting out an all-points for Tracy from the Whale Shark Research Center! Wanted for murder. Out." He releases the button, and we all wait in silence as the radio crackles.

Jamie holds down the button again. "Blond girl from the Whale Shark Research Center, probably carrying a pack. Wanted for murder. Out." The seconds tick by as the radio continues to crackle. Jamie raises the mike to his mouth again just as a voice bursts out of it.

"Ya lookin' for the little blond girl from the Shark Center? Out."

"Roger that," says Jamie anxiously, holding down the button. "She's wanted for murder. Out."

"That you, Jamie Greenfield? Out."

"That's right. Who's this I'm speaking to? Out."

"It's T.J. from Bungie's Café. Ya serious 'bout that murder thing? Out."

At this point I'm ready to rip the mike out of Jamie's hands, but he gives me a warning look.

"It's serious. You seen her? Out."

"Yep. I sure have. Out."

"You want to goddamn tell us where?" I shout, but Jamie doesn't have the button down so my tirade goes unanswered.

Jamie keeps an eye on me as he presses the button. "Where would that be, T.J.? Out."

"She be goin' off in Mr. Christian's boat. Looks like they be headin' for the cays. Out."

"Thank you kindly, T.J. Out."

"Ya tell you' mama to drop round for a coffee sometime, on the house. Out."

"I'll do that. Out."

"We'll take my boat," says Jamie, replacing the mike and heading for the door.

"I need to bring my sister in off the dock," I say, feeling guilty I only just now thought of it. "Is there somewhere I can put her?"

"Bring her in here," says Dr. Jake. "The police should be here soon. They'll need to take a look at her."

I cringe at the thought of strange men pawing over her. If I don't go after Tracy now, it may be too late, but how can I desert my sister? My eyes well up as I think of her alone, not just now but forever. How many times am I going to fail her?

Reesie looks at me worriedly, like she's following the direction of my thoughts. "Do you want I should stay with her?" she asks.

I nod, not trusting myself to speak.

We all go out to the dock. A pelican is perched on the end, close to Pat's body. It flies off when we get close, but following its path upward, I notice several frigate birds circling. They're carrion eaters. I have no doubt why they're hanging around. If I had a rock, I'd throw it at them.

I want to remove the weight belt from Pat's waist, but Dr. Jake says we should leave it for the police to inspect, which makes it a struggle to lift her. She's slippery, and I almost drop her a couple of times, but I won't let anyone help me as I lumber along the dock and back to the office. I lay her gently on the couch and wonder briefly if Dr. Jake would have preferred I put her on the floor, but he claps a reassuring hand on my shoulder.

"I'll take care of the police," he promises. "You go do what you need to do."

Jamie, Zach and I hurry through town to the dock where Jamie keeps his boat. We're a sorry group of heroes, all too aware that any justice we win for Pat now won't achieve the only thing we all want — to have her back. I try to talk to her in my head, but she remains stubbornly silent. I wonder if her voice is lost to me forever. Perhaps she was only trying to lead me to her, or maybe she was never there at all. Maybe it was my imagination from the beginning, and it's only deserted me now because even I'm not deluded enough to conjure a living soul from the stark evidence of her ravaged carcass.

ME: *I know you blame me. I admitted it's my fault. What more can I do?*
PAT:

We clamber into Jamie's boat, a narrow, wooden dory like all the others I've seen here, and cast off from the dock, motoring slowly out of the harbor, picking up speed as we reach open water. The sea looked calm from the shore, but out here the swells are massive. We ride them up eight feet and crash down amid a cascade of water sloshing over the gunwales. Zach rocks with the waves like he's riding a horse, at ease with the rhythm. I clutch the sides of the boat and stare into the dark blue water, wondering why I let him save me from drowning. If I'd stayed with Pat, it would all be over now. Maybe that's all she wanted, company in her final resting place. I'm glad it's too loud for the three of us to talk over the sound of the motor and splashing waves. We're united yet alone, all suffering our own private grief.

The sea smoothes out as we come into a channel between the main island of Utila and the smaller cays off its southwest bank. Though tiny, the island we're approaching seems even more bustling than the town we just left. There are few trees and, apparently, not an inch of undeveloped land. The houses that line the coast are built out into the water on stilts, using the reef as a foundation. Jamie is hailed from shore by several men hurrying along the dock from one of the adjacent buildings.

"She's not here!" one man shouts before we've even docked. "We heard on the radio ya be chasin' down a girl who be goin' with Mr. Christian's boat. They didn't come here." He leans out and catches the rope that Zach throws to him.

"Any idea where they might be?" Jamie asks, steadying the boat with one hand on the dock.

"No. There's been loads of chatter, but no one's seen 'em. I expect Mr. Christian dropped her somewhere and went off to do some fishin'."

"Damn," I mutter. She could be anywhere, and while the radio may be effective for hunting her down on the populated parts of the island, most of the island's just empty forest.

"It's thirty minutes back to town," Jamie says. "We won't hear much until Mr. Christian puts in somewhere, but we could get on the radio so we know where we should be heading."

I exhale in frustration. "That makes sense. We should also radio Reesie and give her an update."

Zach and Jamie nod in agreement so we all pile off the boat and head into the nearest building, which turns out to be a very basic guesthouse for divers. There are a few sticks of furniture and a TV blaring in one corner, with a kid half-asleep in front of it. Other than that, the only modern convenience is a radio. I'm beginning to see how central this apparatus is to remote island living. This one's already crackling away, picking up a conversation between several boats about the location of a school of dolphins. Jamie switches the frequency to the one the Shark Center stands by on and puts in the call.

"This is Jamie, from the cays. Out."

"Hello, Jamie. Dr. Jake at the Shark Center. What are you doing in the cays? Out."

Jamie looks at Zach and me in confusion. We shake our heads.

"We came here looking for Tracy. Out."

"But Reesie got your message you'd gone to Jack Neil. Out."

"What is he talking about?" Jamie asks anxiously.

I take the radio out of his hand. "What message? Out."

"It came in over the radio not more than ten minutes ago. Gudrun from Poppies Hotel sent it. Out."

I raise an eyebrow at Jamie.

"This is Poppies," he explains. "Gudrun is one of the dive masters who works out of here, but their boat was gone when we docked. They must be out diving already."

"Gudrun said Tracy'd been dropped at Jack Neil Beach, so Reesie left in the dinghy twenty minutes ago and went to meet you there. Out," says Dr. Jake.

"Where's Jack Neil Beach?" I ask with a flash of hope. But Jamie doesn't answer as he turns to the kid lounging in front of the TV.

"Has Gudrun been on the radio this morning?"

The kid looks over at us in surprise. "Not from here. She took a group out early. She could have called from the boat, though."

"We've got to go," Jamie says over his shoulder, already racing for the door with Zach behind him. I see them through the window, sprinting hell-bent along the dock, so I tear after them. Something is clearly wrong. My stomach churns when I realize it somehow involves Reesie.

Jamie and Zach have the boat untied and the motor going by the time I'm clambering into it.

"If Gudrun had sent the message, she would have said she was calling from the *Ol' Tom*; that's the name of their boat. She wouldn't have said she was calling from Poppies," Zach explains, as Jamie focuses on hot-rodding out of the harbor without crashing into anyone.

I'm still confused. "Maybe Dr. Jake was talking about where she worked, not where she was calling from."

"People here don't make that kind of mistake," Zach replies. "A lot of places on and around this island have no telephone reception. The radio is the only way to communicate. If there's a crisis — an earthquake, an accident, a swamped ship — the radio is the only thing standing between them and death. They get on it; they identify their location. It's the first thing they do. Always."

"So you're saying Gudrun didn't send that message?"

"Exactamundo," Zach says.

CHAPTER 21

It's an excruciating fifteen minutes to Jack Neil Beach, halfway back in the direction of town. Jamie takes the waves as quickly as we can. Several times I think we're going to capsize, but finally we round the last headland. Zach leaps to his feet and excitedly points out Jack Neil dock. I am so relieved to see Reesie lying on the end, but my heart thumps when she struggles to sit up, only to flop back down, raising her arm in a feeble wave. As we get closer, we can see the blood oozing from the side of her head.

I'm up and off the boat before Jamie's even cut the motor. I run to Reesie and kneel down, pull off my T-shirt in a fluid motion and press it to the wound.

"I'm sorry," she gasps. "Tracy —"

"Not now, Reesie," I cut her off. "You need to lie still."

She struggles to sit up, pushing away my restraining hand.

Jamie's right behind me and drops to his knees, picking up the T-shirt Reesie has cast off and struggling to hold her down while I press it against the wound again.

"Calm yourself, girl," he commands.

"Tracy's getting away!" she gasps urgently. "She stole the dinghy. She was hiding. We've got to —"

"For once in your life, you are not the one giving orders here," snaps Jamie. "Zach, go down the beach to Mr. Wolfe. It's the round gray house. Get on to Dr. Jake and tell him we need a fast boat to town."

Zach hurtles down the dock before Jamie finishes his instructions.

"She's heading for Ceiba," Reesie moans. "She's trying to leave the country. You have to listen to me."

"Luke," Jamie says. "It's up to you. I've got to stay with Reesie. Take my boat; it's a damn sight faster than the dinghy. You might be able to catch her."

I look at him in horror and glance over at his boat. I've never driven a boat before. But I can't let my sister's murderer just get away. I search the shoreline, wondering how long it will be before Zach returns. I can't even see him. He disappeared into the trees the second he left the dock. He may not have gotten that far, but am I really prepared to wait? Every second could mean the difference between catching up with Tracy and letting her escape. I realize I don't have a choice.

"The key's still in the motor," says Jamie. "Just keep your sights on Pico Bonito and head straight for it." He nods at the distant shore, where the silhouette of a steep, conical mountain disappears into the clouds.

I nod briskly but don't speak. I know my voice will betray my fear. My entire body quivering, I force myself to stride steadily over to the boat. I climb in and turn the key. The motor jumps to life. Just like driving a car. I turn the throttle and the boat starts to move. Unfortunately, the dock starts to move with it.

"The ropes," Jamie yells, scuttling over to untie the one closest to him. I turn off the motor and scramble across the bow to untie the other one.

"Just practicing," I say sheepishly.

"He's going to get himself killed," says Reesie, moaning as she tries to sit up. "This is a bad plan, Jamie."

Jamie returns to her side and I repeat the steps of turning on the engine. This time when I give it juice, it rockets away from the dock like it might go airborne.

"Don't be giving it too much throttle," Jamie calls after me, but I can barely hear him over the roar of the engine as I hurtle toward the wide-open sea.

In a twelve-foot boat.

With no radio.

And a useless cell phone that can't get reception.

In at least one hundred feet of water.

Now five hundred.

One thousand.

Sharks can attack in less than two feet of water.

Is that supposed to be reassuring?

This was a mistake.

But I have to catch Tracy.

Focus on the mountain.

How big is that wave?

Holy crap.

———

Water sluices over me, drenching my clothes and filling the boat. I scrabble at my feet with one hand, keeping the other on the throttle. There's some kind of plastic jug beneath my seat. I yank it out and am relieved to see it's an empty milk jug with the top sliced off, perfect for bailing. I fling water out of the boat as fast as I can, but it's a losing battle as an onslaught of waves, three in a row, crash over the bow, sending torrents of water back in my face. My eyes sting from the salt; I can hardly keep them open. I squint at Pico Bonito for brief seconds in between squeezing my eyes shut, hoping my own tears will clear the salt. I continue hurtling forward, but the mountain never gets any closer. Only the land behind me recedes. I can no longer make out the dock or distinguish trees from the hazy green outline of the little island I've left. Still I keep going until Utila disappears completely. The mainland remains an indistinct smudge on the horizon.

In one of my peeks through burning eyes, I think I see something moving just ahead.

Another quick look confirms it.

A fin? I saw a dorsal.

My heart pounds so hard, I think it's going to burst through my rib cage.

I force my eyes wide open, though they're streaming so badly I'm nearly blind. I look around and there they are, three dorsals off the starboard bow.

And then I see more.

At least a dozen.

Double that.

Triple.

There are hundreds of them. I'm surrounded. One of the creatures leaps out of the water, spins twice and crashes back into the sea. This starts a craze and they all start doing it, leaping and spinning, in unison and alone. The sea churns with their riotous dance.

Not sharks.

Dolphins.

They know I'm here, I'm certain of it. It's not only that some pop up and look at me, leap so close I fear they'll tumble into the boat; it's more than that. They're doing this for my benefit, showing off like rowdy street urchins, proving how completely they own this expanse of ocean. As I watch them, I forget my stinging eyes, my cold goose-pimpled body, and wish more than anything that I could join them.

ME: *This is where you belonged, Pat. When Mom took the pills, it destroyed what was best in you — your relentless hope, your belief that you could create a future that was better than our past. I couldn't let that happen.*

PAT:

The dolphins are moving off, still twirling, taunting me to follow, share in their exuberance of life and each other. I lean dangerously over the side of the boat, my entire being craning toward them, but I let them go, too.

Once again, I'm alone.

Ocean surrounds me, stretching out in every direction, slate gray, reflecting the sky and my mood.

At first, there's just a speck on the horizon, bobbing in and out of sight as it climbs the waves and disappears behind them. But as I close the distance, I can make out the outline of another boat, a small one with a single passenger. Time slows down as the image becomes clearer, blond hair whipping out behind narrow, hunched shoulders. She leans into the wind, her back to me, but her compact, wiry frame, the calm sureness of her movements, are etched into me like a tattoo. I would know her anywhere — my sister's killer.

She hears me at the last minute, over the wind and her preoccupation with her own single-minded flight. Turning, she reaches for something on the seat beside her.

A speargun.

She points it at me, cutting her motor at the same time, so she can use both hands to steady it.

"Not very sporting of you, Tracy," I shout, pulling up on her left side, but keeping some distance between us. "I thought fish-huggers didn't go in for equipment like that."

"It's only for emergencies," she calls back. "I'd say this qualifies."

"You only have one spear. What if you miss?"

"I won't miss."

"I can't let you get away. You'll have to kill me."

"If that's what you want."

She leans into the gun, closing one eye as she aims. I give the engine full throttle in the same instant the arrow takes flight. It grazes my shoulder, taking my breath away before continuing its trajectory across the stern and into the water beyond. I put my hand up to my wound. It feels deep and hurts like hell. I'm just glad it's my left arm as I give the throttle a hard jerk to the right and charge straight for the dinghy. The impact throws Tracy into the water and would do the same for me if I wasn't hunkered down ready for it. She disappears for a moment, and I wonder if she's gone under my boat. Her own is bobbing upside down on the waves, but from the size of the hole in its side, it isn't going to be there long. My engine died on impact. I hope I can get it started again.

Tracy breaks the surface a few feet from her boat, spitting water. "Are you nuts?" she shrieks. "You could have killed us both!"

"And that would be worse than you killing me?"

She strokes over to my boat and reaches one hand up, grasping the gunwale. "Pull me in, asshole."

I prime the motor, advance the throttle and pull the handle, relieved when the engine turns over almost immediately. I'm not planning to leave her here, but I'm not in any hurry to help her either.

She reaches her other hand up and starts pulling and shimmying her way up the side. The boat sits high in the water, and she falls back a couple of times in frustration while I continue to watch. She keeps at it until she's swung one leg up and over; the girl's got good upper body strength. I'm tempted to push her back down, but I can't do it. She was the only one with Pat at the end and I need answers.

She flops on the deck of the boat, gasping, while I scramble over her to grab Jamie's carpenter's belt. I noticed it earlier, stowed in the bow, and I don't want her coming at me with a hammer. I just want to get my business done with her so I can get her out of my sight. The sooner I turn her over to the police, the better.

Finally, she hauls herself up onto one of the seats and glares at me. "Why couldn't you have followed your dick like a normal guy?"

"I beg your pardon?"

"You know — when I came on to you. If we'd slept together, it wouldn't have occurred to you to suspect me."

"I think you overestimate the power of your sexual attraction."

She rolls her eyes. "Guys are all the same. I had Pete believing I loved him and was actually trying to help him, when all the time I was setting him up."

"It was you planting the dolls, wasn't it?"

"Of course." She smirks, but it turns into a grimace. "A fat lot of good it did me. That should have had you going after Jamie."

"Where did you get voodoo dolls?"

She snickers. "They weren't voodoo dolls, just cloth dolls. They sell them at the Guatemalan store at the edge of town. I thought for sure someone would catch on to that."

I take a deep breath, steeling myself to ask the only question I really care about.

"Why did you kill her?"

Tracy shrugs and pulls off her shirt. For a minute I think this is another attempt at seduction, but she just wrings it out and lays it over the bench between us to dry. The wind has dropped, and the sun emerges from behind the clouds. She slides down to the deck, stretches her legs toward me, leans back against the middle bench and closes her eyes for several minutes. I'm beginning to think she's fallen asleep, so it startles me when she answers my question.

"It's not like I planned it," she murmurs. "Pete was my boyfriend, but like I told you, that was over the minute he met your sister. The night she died, we were all at the bar. Your sister was upset about something, drinking more than she normally did. Pete was doing his best to take advantage of that, but she still wasn't interested. When she started talking about going back to the room, I took off first. I wanted to spy on them, see how she'd behave if she thought they were alone. I figured maybe Pete was right and she was playing hard to get. Without me around, maybe she'd give in to him and that would have suited me fine. She could have Pete. I liked Jamie better anyway. I was already planning how I'd break the news to him about his slutty girlfriend. I watched them go down to the dock. Your sister said she wanted to be alone, but she had to know Pete wouldn't go for that. She was leading him on, if you ask me, but when he tried to kiss her, she put up a fight. Then she fell, just like he said."

Tracy's mouth curves into a smile as she remembers this part. "I was so excited. I thought he'd killed her. But when he went into the office to call for help, I ran down and checked and she was still breathing." She opens her eyes, glances at me and straightens up. "That's when I thought of it. It just came to me, the solution to everything — and it was so easy. How could I resist? You have to understand; your sister was a royal bitch."

My fists clench. "Then what happened?"

"I ran to the equipment room and got a weight belt, strapped it on her and rolled her off the dock. I was back in my room pretending to be asleep by the time Pete returned. He didn't know what had happened. He came knocking on my door, sobbing out the whole story. What a loser!" She laughs.

"Did Pat struggle when she went in the water?" I don't know why I ask this. The rage coiled within me is already more than I can bear. I don't want to know that my sister suffered. I don't want to hear that she fought for her life. I'm not sure I can handle it. Yet, at the same time, I feel I owe it to Pat to hear it. All I can do for her now is bear witness to her story.

Tracy begins untying her sneakers. They're sopping wet and the knots don't come loose easily.

"Tracy, did my sister know what was happening?"

She shoots me a guilty look and resumes picking at her shoelace. In that glance, I have my answer. I leap across the bench that separates us. Before I know it, my hands are around her throat, squeezing tight. It's like I'm watching myself but feeling every sensation at the same time — the softness of her skin, the resilience of her flesh as she struggles to draw breath, the panic in her eyes.

"Ook," she sputters.

Pat: *Let her go!*

I leap up, drop Tracy, and her body slides to the deck of the boat.

Did I imagine that?

Me: *Pat?*

"Pat!?" I scream, sweeping the horizon in every direction.

Eventually, my gaze falls on Tracy, just Tracy, pale but still breathing, glaring up at me.

"You're crazy," she rasps.

I slump down on the nearest bench, struggling for breath myself.

"Tell me about the end," I say quietly.

She rubs her throat, eyeing me reproachfully. I'm in the middle of the boat now, so she clambers forward to take the bench farthest from me, in the bow.

"I didn't realize she was conscious until she hit the water," she says, but I can tell by the way her eyes slide off me, she's lying. "The water must have woken her up. She thrashed about. Maybe she was trying to get the weight belt off, I don't know. It was dark. But the bitch just wouldn't die. Even at the end, she had to be so goddamn perfect."

She stops and looks past me, as if she's seeing it all over again. Now I can see it, too. The harbor lights play across the water, sparkling on my sister's hair as she breaches the surface, scrabbling at her waist, trying desperately to free herself. Blood pulses out of the wound on her head, clouding the water like the ink of an octopus. She goes under twice, three times, but still she doesn't give up; she begins swimming for shore, hauling the extra weight. She's weakened but still strong, and she's in her element, her home.

"You finished her off," I say flatly. I don't know how she did it, but I know that much.

"I hit her with the anchor," she says. "I had to. I'd already put the belt on her. There was no going back. She would have told. So I got the anchor out of the dinghy and slung it at her head. She went down after that . . . finally."

CHAPTER 22

Everyone — Zach, Jamie, even Reesie with a bandaged head — is standing on the dock when we pull in after a long, wordless journey. Stunned into silence by Tracy's confession, I want nothing more than to be out of her presence. It's as if her malignance is infectious. I feel tainted just being close to her and can only be cleansed by seeing my sister. I know, in reality, there's nothing of Pat in the remains I pulled from the sea, but it's all I've got. Pat and I have unfinished business, one final conversation we need to have. I heard her voice out on the water. She, too, has been silent on the boat ride back, but perhaps if I can be alone with her one more time, she'll say the words I need to hear.

The police are waiting on the shore with Dr. Jake. From the excitement with which they greet our arrival, they must have been told about Tracy. I toss out the bow rope to Jamie and he ties us up. I wait for Tracy to scramble up on the dock before I follow. I don't know where she'd escape to, with so many observers, but I'm not taking any chances.

"She confessed," I say, as I climb up beside my friends.

"You can't prove it," she says belligerently, though her voice cracks. "I'll deny everything."

"We'll see about that," says Reesie. "Patricia was one of us. We're gonna make sure justice is done — one way or another."

"Where's Pat?" I ask.

"She's still inside," says Reesie. "The police have finished their examination, so we need to talk about arrangements. I imagine you'll be wanting to take her home."

I nod. I know I'm going to have to call my parents again. The prospect fills me with dread, though I hold on to a faint hope that at least getting Pat's body back will give them some comfort. I've already resolved to do everything in my power to hide from them the full truth of her final moments. It's enough that I have to live with it.

"You need to come to the station to give your statement," says Jamie. "Do you want a minute with Pat first? I can hand Tracy over." He already has a firm grip on her arm.

I nod again, not trusting myself to speak. The adrenaline that carried me through the past hour, chasing Tracy on the high seas and bringing her back, has dissipated, leaving me shaky and close to breaking down. Jamie precedes me off the dock, dragging Tracy along with him. Reesie and Zach follow me. I pause briefly at the end of the dock to exchange a few words with Dr. Jake, who seems overcome with emotion that so much evil has been perpetrated on his watch. I try to reassure him he's not responsible, but I think he takes my obvious preoccupation for lack of conviction, not realizing that I'm thinking of my own guilt, not his.

Zach and Reesie come with me into the Shark Center. They wait just outside the office, letting me go in alone.

I sit down on the edge of the sofa, next to my sister, and take her hand.

"I caught Tracy," I tell her, listening for her response with every ounce of my being. But catching Tracy doesn't give Pat her life back. I can hardly expect gratitude.

"I'm sorry I wrote the letter applying for the job at the Shark Center." I thought it would be a relief to finally admit this out loud but, in the end, it just seems superfluous, like catching Tracy; it doesn't change anything. "You must have known I wrote it. It wasn't easy sending it from your e-mail account. It took more than my usual tricks to figure out your password. But pretending to be you, actually writing the application, was effortless. In fact, once I started writing about your passion for the sea, everything you'd done and achieved seemed to build naturally to you working at the Shark Center. I'm surprised you didn't think of it yourself. But that was the problem. You weren't thinking about what was best for you anymore. You'd stopped dreaming about your future. It felt like my fear had finally infected you. I need you to forgive me, Pat."

"She knew it was you, Luke," says Jamie. I jump and whip round. How long has he been standing there?

"You were right," he continues. "When your mom took the pills, Trish got scared. She'd decided to stick around and look after your mom, but you changed her mind. When she got the reply from the Shark Center, she read the letter you wrote pretending to be her. She saw herself through your eyes and realized how much you wanted her to fulfill her dream. But she saw something else, too."

"Yeah, what was that?"

"You didn't need her anymore. Maybe you never had. It took a lot of courage to let her go."

"But I got her killed. If I'd been the brother she needed, she never would have thought of staying home in the first place. She would have trusted me to pick up the slack when she went off to college. It turned out to be a bad idea, but the whale shark research program was the only thing I could find that sounded tempting enough to lure her away."

"You see, that's where you're wrong," says Zach, squeezing past Jamie to enter the room. It makes me wonder if Reesie's out there eavesdropping as well. Seconds after, she follows Zach in and plops down on the floor at my feet.

"Tricia belonged here," Zach continues. "The internship and this island weren't a consolation prize. They were everything she'd ever wanted, and you made it happen. You can't let Tracy's actions make you doubt the really wonderful thing you did. Tracy's twisted stuff could have happened anywhere. Life's just risky, man, and there are a lot of cold people out there. Don't get down on yourself. I may not have much family experience, but you're the first person I've ever met who I wished was my family."

I look away in embarrassment, but when I turn back, he's watching me intently. I stand up and pull him into a hug before pushing him away and punching him in the arm. He grins.

"What's this shit you're talking?" I say gruffly. "We've already established we're brothers. You don't think you're getting out of that, do you? In fact, I've been thinking maybe you'd help me take Pat home."

"Really?" A gleam of hope springs into his eyes so I know I'm on the right track, even though I don't know what the heck my parents are going to do when I show up with a new sibling.

"Absolutely," I say. "You could stay with us for a while. We could finish high school together, maybe even go to college. I could use a study buddy. I'm not sure I have a great track record for deciding what's best for people, but I think it's where *you* belong."

He grins so big now, he's nothing but teeth.

"Cosmic," he says and holds out his knuckles so I can rap them with my own.

I turn back to my sister.

Me: *I don't know if you're angry at me, Pat, or if it's like Martha said, it's just time for you to move on. But I hope somewhere you're watching because, even if you're not in my head anymore, you'll always be in my heart and I'm going to make you proud.*

Pat:

EPILOGUE

I secure the container under the gunwale and clamber to the back of the boat to start the motor.

The whale sharks are on the north side of the island, the side opposite from the town and harbor. The water is much deeper there and rougher, though it's the depth that appeals to the sharks. I've been many times in the month that I've been working at the Whale Shark Research Center, but this is the first time I'm going on my own. Jamie's dory is a lot smaller than the research boat I'm used to, so a ripple of apprehension surges through me. Still, I've gotten good at facing my fears in the year since Pat's death. It's a lot harder than drowning them in booze.

I round the bend of the island where the sea grass goes out right to the drop-off. Then I'm off the North Shore, with its steep volcanic cliffs and crashing waves drowning out even the sound of the motor. I angle the boat away from shore, heading for indigo water. A shark can attack in less than two feet of water, so it's pointless panicking just because it's deep. Floating atop miles of ocean still freaks me out, though. I scan the horizon, looking for the cluster of seabirds that will give away the location of a boil of fish that means whale shark.

I'm lucky. After thirty minutes of motoring straight out into ever deeper water, I spot a flock of birds circling and diving. I head for them at full speed. I'm worried there won't be a shark and equally nervous there will be. Even after a month of chasing them, I can't get used to their size and power. I debate whether I actually need to find a whale shark. I don't want to run out of gas and get stuck out here. Maybe the open ocean would be good enough. But Pat loved the sharks, and this is her journey. I know what she'd want. I know what I have to do.

If it's not a whale shark, I'll keep looking. I'm almost on top of the boil before a fin breaks the surface, rising at least five feet. The shark is huge, the biggest I've seen at three times the length of my boat. My heart starts fluttering, and I have to remind myself that it won't hurt me. I take a deep breath and turn off my motor. I need my hands free for what I'm about to do and, unlike the research boat, Jamie's dory doesn't have an air-powered motor and I don't want to slice the shark with my propeller.

I climb over the benches to the front of the boat, keeping one eye on the fin that I swear is moving closer, though that might be my paranoia. Reaching under the gunwale, I pull out the jar that contains my sister, or what's left of her. I wish it was a more fitting container. We had her in a silver urn at home, but it didn't close securely, so I had to transfer her to a mason jar for the trip back to Utila.

The fin has definitely approached, and I'm not being paranoid when I say it's making wide, sweeping circles around my boat. I spread my legs to steady myself as I stand up and unscrew the lid of Pat's jar. I'm out of the habit of talking to her and there's no one else here, so I just hold the jar aloft — and practically drop it when a huge mouth appears less than two feet away. I know it's not going to eat me, but this close, it could definitely capsize the boat. I plop down again and try to slow my breathing.

PAT: *Are we going to do this or what?*

I leap to my feet and look around. I'm alone, but I can hear her voice as clearly as I ever could.

ME: *Pat?*

PAT: *No, it's the shark talking. Who do you think it is, moron?*

ME: *You know I'm about to feed your earthly remains to a sixty-foot predator.*

I glower at the jar.

PAT: *I sure as hell hope so. I was afraid you might have chickened out.*

ME: *Really? You think I'm chicken? You don't know the half of what I've done this year.*

PAT: *You brought me back here. That's all I need to know.*

I hold my sister aloft.

ME: *Are you ready to be one with the fish?*

PAT: *I've been ready my whole life.*

The shark has started circling again. As I tip the jar and the first grains of ash hit the water, a glistening face pops up to watch the spectacle. Bits of my sister disperse through the waves, catching on the snout of the shark and sinking to the depths below. I watch as a remora dives into the stream of her and lean out over the side so I can follow her journey. The last bits of her catch the sunlight and sparkle as they descend into the vastness of the world she loved.

Praise for *An Infidel in Paradise*
by S.J. Laidlaw

"Laidlaw, a globetrotting social worker, puts her firsthand knowledge of faraway lands and cultures to good use in this exciting tale of a Canadian teen's encounters with some of the best and worst features of a radically different society. Emma's first-person, present-tense narration is realistic and compelling." — *VOYA*

"This is an honest and realistic story about being an outsider in another country. . . . Laidlaw does not hold back from depicting some of the less-attractive aspects of Pakistani life, but she also conveys a sense of beauty and wonder of this culture."

— *School Library Journal*

"*An Infidel in Paradise* is a very well-written evocation of both a tormented teen and the exotic setting she finds herself in . . . teen readers will relate to Emma's struggles and learn much from this excellent portrayal of culture clash." — *Quill & Quire*

"Laidlaw has created a rich and layered text. Readers see Emma and her world through multiple lenses: teenager, diplomat, Canadian. Her descriptions of both the very rich and the very poor communities of Islamabad are carefully and respectfully drawn. Seeing this world through the eyes of a teenager gives the reader the opportunity to explore the differences in a very engaging way. . . . Highly Recommended." — *CM Magazine*

"I hope every teen reads this book and that everyone who knows a teen reads it. *An Infidel in Paradise* was a pleasure to read (even if it did make me cry more than once), and I will definitely be keeping my eye out for more work by S.J. Laidlaw."

— *About.com*